National Wall Paper Co.

Catalogue of window shades and shade hardware, paper hangers

tools and supplies.

National Wall Paper Co.

Catalogue of window shades and shade hardware, paper hangers tools and supplies.

ISBN/EAN: 9783741193361

Manufactured in Europe, USA, Canada, Australia, Japa

Cover: Foto ©Andreas Hilbeck / pixelio.de

Manufactured and distributed by brebook publishing software (www.brebook.com)

ILLUSTRATED CATALOGUE

—OF—

WINDOW * SHADES * AND * SHADE * GOODS,

VESTIBULE HARDWARE,

Upholstery Goods, Paper-Hangers' Supplies, and Shade-Makers' Tools,

—FROM—

NEW YORK JOBBING BRANCH,

NATIONAL WALL PAPER CO.,

JOBBERS EXCLUSIVELY OF

Wall Paper and Window Shades,

416-422 BROOME STREET, COR. ELM STREET,

NEW YORK.

WE wish you to understand that we handle only the BEST QUALITY and MAKE of the different grades of SHADE MATERIAL, and prices quoted are for perfect goods. Should Competition make it necessary to lower our prices, you will get the benefit; or, if any change in cost of manufacture makes it necessary to advance prices, we claim the right to do so, but remember you will always be sold the goods at lowest market quotations.

NEW YORK JOBBING BRANCH,
NATIONAL WALL PAPER COMPANY.

National Wall Paper Co.

Catalogue of window shades and shade hardware, paper hangers tools and supplies.

SHADE DEPARTMENT.

TERMS.

If Paid in 10 Days, Two Per Cent. Discount.

If Paid in 30 Days, One Per Cent. Discount.

Longest Time Allowed, 60 Days, Net.

PRICES SUBJECT TO CHANGE WITHOUT NOTICE.

PARTIES HAVING NO ACCOUNT WITH US WILL PLEASE SEND REFERENCES
WITH ORDER, THAT THERE MAY BE NO DELAY IN MAKING SHIPMENT.

NEW YORK REFERENCES PREFERRED.

All Claims must be made AT ONCE upon Receipt of Goods, and must set forth Date, Book,
Page and Order Number, as shown by Invoices.

WE SEND UNDER THIS COVER

OUR SECOND ANNUAL CATALOGUE OF

Plain and Decorated Mounted Window Shades,

⇒ SHADE, UPHOLSTERY AND VESTIBULE HARDWARE ⇒

Wall Paper Devices and Paper Hangers's Tools.

We want to impress upon you the fact that we deal exclusively in Wall Paper and Shade Goods, and by making your selection from this list you may feel sure you are buying the right goods and buying them at right prices, and in ordering by number you will save very much time, annoyance and expense. Keep this list lying on your counter, and refer to it for whatever you want in this line, allowing your customers to consult it freely. By the arrangement as shown by the perforated slip in front of book, you may make this Catalogue do duty as a very superior salesman.

CHANGES IN PRICES.

We desire to distinctly impress upon those who receive this Catalogue, that "All prices are subject to change without notice."

IMPORTANT SUGGESTIONS.

State particularly how to ship goods, whether by freight, express or mail. Goods sent by mail are always at risk of purchaser. Our responsibility on freight and express shipments ceases when we deliver goods to the transportation company.

Goods sent as ordered cannot be taken back.

In checking a bill of goods, open every paper box, as it is often convenient to pack several articles of a different description under a cover designed for one.

Please destroy your Shade Catalogue No. 1 for 1894, and order from this.
Order by number and descriptions given, and do not mutilate Catalogue.

Respectfully,

NEW YORK JOBBING BRANCH,

NATIONAL WALL PAPER CO.

January 15th, 1895.

PLAIN MOUNTED WINDOW SHADES.

Mounted on Spring Stop Rollers, ready to hang. Lengths given are for cloth before hemming and mounting.
Priced and sold by the dozen. We do not break dozen packages.

"BROOKLYN" FELTS.

A good, cheap shade.

No.	Color	Length	Per Doz.
5156	Olive Green	6 feet	$2.80
5157	" "	7 "	3.04
5286	Pea Green	6 "	2.80
5287	" "	7 "	3.04
5566	Medium Drab	6 "	2.80
5567	" "	7 "	3.04
5646	Dark Spanish Olive	6 "	2.80
5647	" "	7 "	3.04
5666	Light " "	6 "	2.80
5667	" "	7 "	3.04
5376	Spanish Olive	6 "	2.80
5377	" "	7 "	3.04

"CRITERION" GLAZED HOLLAND.

Warranted best quality made.

No.	Color	Length	Per Doz.
806	Cardinal	6 feet	$5.00
807	"	7 "	5.70
816	Brown	6 "	5.00
817	"	7 "	5.70
826	Slate	6 "	5.00
827	"	7 "	5.70
836	Ecru	6 "	5.00
837	"	7 "	5.70
846	Drab	6 "	5.00
847	"	7 "	5.70
856	Green	6 "	5.00
857	"	7 "	5.70
866	Blue	6 "	5.00
867	"	7 "	5.70
876	Nile	6 "	5.00
877	"	7 "	5.70
886	Spanish Olive	6 "	5.00
887	" "	7 "	5.70

"ONTARIO" WATER COLORED OPAQUE.

No.	Color	Length	Per Doz.
2056	Light Blue	6 feet	$5.50
2057	" "	7 "	6.20
2156	Olive Green	6 "	5.50
2157	" "	7 "	6.20
2266	Terra Cotta	6 "	5.50
2267	" "	7 "	6.20
2326	Medium Stone	6 "	5.50
2327	" "	7 "	6.20
2386	Light Pea Green	6 "	5.50
2387	" "	7 "	6.20
2566	Medium Drab	6 "	5.50
2567	" "	7 "	6.20
2586	Naples Tint	6 "	5.50
2587	" "	7 "	6.20
2646	Dark Spanish Olive	6 "	5.50
2647	" "	7 "	6.20
2666	Light Spanish Olive	6 "	5.50
2667	" "	7 "	6.20
2686	Ecru	6 "	5.60
2687	" "	7 "	6.20

"SENECA" OIL PAINTED OPAQUE.

No.	Color	Length	Per Doz.
1056	Light Blue	6 feet	$6.60
1057	" "	7 "	7.00
1156	Olive Green	6 "	6.60
1157	"	7 "	7.00
1266	Terra Cotta	6 "	6.60
1267	"	7 "	7.00
1326	Medium Stone	6 "	6.60
1327	"	7 "	7.00
1386	Light Pea Green	6 "	6.60
1387	" "	7 "	7.00
1566	Medium Drab	6 "	6.60
1567	"	7 "	7.00
1586	Naples Tint	6 "	6.60
1587	" "	7 "	7.00
1646	Dark Spanish Olive	6 "	6.60
1647	" "	7 "	7.00
1666	Light " "	6 "	6.60
1667	" "	7 "	7.00
1686	Ecru	6 "	6.60
1687	"	7 "	7.00

"MINETTO" OIL PAINTED OPAQUE.

The best quality of machine-finished Goods.

No.	Color	Length	Per Doz.
615	Olive Green	6 feet	$7.20
715	"	7 "	8.20
634	Dark Stone	6 "	7.20
734	"	7 "	8.20
638	Light Pea Green	6 "	7.20
738	" "	7 "	8.20
652	Fawn	6 "	7.20
752	"	7 "	8.20
656	Medium Drab	6 "	7.20
756	"	7 "	8.20
658	Naples Tint	6 "	7.20
758	"	7 "	8.20
664	Dark Spanish Olive	6 "	7.20
764	" "	7 "	8.20
666	Light " "	6 "	7.20
766	"	7 "	8.20
668	Ecru	6 "	7.20
768	"	7 "	8.20
674	Salmon	6 "	7.20
774	"	7 "	8.20

LONSDALE HOLLAND.

Best American made Goods.

No.	Color	Length	Per Doz.
706	White	6 feet	$9.60
707	"	7 "	11.00
716	Brown, No. 21	6 "	10.30
717	"	7 "	11.70
726	Light Drab, No. 20	6 "	10.30
727	"	7 "	11.70
786	Buff, No. 19	6 "	10.30
787	"	7 "	11.70
746	Green	6 "	10.30
747	"	7 "	11.70
756	Ecru, No. 16	6 "	10.30
757	"	7 "	11.70

"Small" sample books showing qualities and colors in above materials furnished on application.

SEE PERFORATED SLIP AND FRONT PAGES FOR DISCOUNT AND TERMS.

PLAIN FRINGED MOUNTED WINDOW SHADES.

Mounted on Spring Stop Rollers, ready to hang. Lengths given are for cloth before hemming and mounting.
Priced and sold by the dozen. We do not break dozen packages.

"BROOKLYN" FELTS.

Finished with No. 480 Fringe.

No.	Color.	Length.	Per Doz.
F5156	Olive Green	6 feet	$3.60
F5157	" "	7 "	3.84
F5386	Pea Green	6 "	3.60
F5387	" "	7 "	3.84
F5566	Medium Drab	6 "	3.60
F5567	" "	7 "	3.84
F5646	Dark Spanish Olive	6 "	3.60
F5647	" "	7 "	3.84
F5666	Light " "	6 "	3.60
F5667	" "	7 "	3.84
F5876	Spanish Olive	6 "	3.60
F5877	" "	7 "	3.84

"ONTARIO" OPAQUES.

Finished with No. 480 Fringe.

No.	Color.	Length.	Per Doz.
F2056	Light Blue	6 feet	$6.30
F2057	" "	7 "	7.00
F2156	Olive Green	6 "	6.30
F2157	" "	7 "	7.00
F2266	Terra Cotta	6 "	6.30
F2267	" "	7 "	7.00
F2326	Medium Stone	6 "	6.30
F2327	" "	7 "	7.00
F2386	Pea Green	6 "	6.30
F2387	" "	7 "	7.00
F2566	Medium Drab	6 "	6.30
F2567	" "	7 "	7.00
F2586	Naples Tint	6 "	6.30
F2587	" "	7 "	7.00
F2646	Dark Spanish Olive	6 "	6.30
F2647	" "	7 "	7.00
F2666	Light Spanish Olive	6 "	6.30
F2667	" "	7 "	7.00
F2686	Ecru	6 "	6.30
F2687	" "	7 "	7.00

Finished with No. 425 Fringe.

No.	Color.	Length.	Per Doz.
K2056	Electric Blue	6 feet	$7.70
K2057	" "	7 "	8.40
K2156	Olive Green	6 "	7.70
K2157	" "	7 "	8.40
K2266	Terra Cotta	6 "	7.70
K2267	" "	7 "	8.40
K2326	Medium Stone	6 "	7.70
K2327	" "	7 "	8.40
K2386	Pea Green	6 "	7.70
K2387	" "	7 "	8.40
K2586	Naples Tint	6 "	7.70
K2587	" "	7 "	8.40
K2646	Dark Spanish Olive	6 "	7.70
K2647	" "	7 "	8.40
K2666	Light " "	6 "	7.70
K2667	" "	7 "	8.40
K2686	Ecru	6 "	7.70
K2687	" "	7 "	8.40

"ONTARIO" OPAQUES.—Continued.

Finished with "M" Fringe.

No.	Color.	Length.	Per Doz.
M2056	Light Blue	6 feet	$11.50
M2057	" "	7 "	12.20
M2156	Olive Green	6 "	11.50
M2157	" "	7 "	12.20
M2266	Terra Cotta	6 "	11.50
M2267	" "	7 "	12.20
M2326	Medium Stone	6 "	11.50
M2327	" "	7 "	12.20
M2386	Pea Green	6 "	11.50
M2387	" "	7 "	12.20
M2566	Medium Drab	6 "	11.50
M2567	" "	7 "	12.20
M2586	Naples Tint	6 "	11.50
M2587	" "	7 "	12.20
M2646	Dark Spanish Olive	6 "	11.50
M2647	" "	7 "	12.20
M2666	Light " "	6 "	11.50
M2667	" "	7 "	12.20
M2686	Ecru	6 "	11.50
M2687	" "	7 "	12.20

"SENECA" OPAQUES.

Finished with No. 64 Fringe.

No.	Color.	Length.	Per Doz.
F1056	Light Blue	6 feet	$8.20
F1057	" "	7 "	9.20
F1156	Olive Green	6 "	8.20
F1157	" "	7 "	9.20
F1266	Terra Cotta	6 "	8.20
F1267	" "	7 "	9.20
F1326	Medium Stone	6 "	8.20
F1327	" "	7 "	9.20
F1386	Pea Green	6 "	8.20
F1387	" "	7 "	9.20
F1566	Medium Drab	6 "	8.20
F1567	" "	7 "	9.20
F1586	Naples Tint	6 "	8.20
F1587	" "	7 "	9.20
F1646	Dark Spanish Olive	6 "	8.20
F1647	" "	7 "	9.20
F1666	Light " "	6 "	8.20
F1667	" "	7 "	9.20
F1686	Ecru	6 "	8.20
F1687	" "	7 "	9.20

Finished with No. 2070 Fringe.

No.	Color.	Length.	Per Doz.
L1056	Light Blue	6 feet	$9.80
L1057	" "	7 "	10.80
L1156	Olive Green	6 "	9.80
L1157	" "	7 "	10.80
L1266	Terra Cotta	6 "	9.80
L1267	" "	7 "	10.80
L1326	Medium Stone	6 "	9.80
L1327	" "	7 "	10.80
L1386	Pea Green	6 "	9.80
L1387	" "	7 "	10.80
L1566	Medium Drab	6 "	9.80
L1567	" "	7 "	10.80
L1586	Naples Tint	6 "	9.80
L1587	" "	7 "	10.80
L1646	Dark Spanish Olive	6 "	9.80
L1647	" "	7 "	10.80
L1666	Light " "	6 "	9.80
L1667	" "	7 "	10.80
L1686	Ecru	6 "	9.80
L1687	" "	7 "	10.80

For cuts and descriptions of fringes see pages 38 to 39.
Sample books showing colors and qualities of above materials mailed on application.

DECORATED MOUNTED **WINDOW** SHADES.

Mounted upon spring stop rollers, ready to hang.   Lengths given are for cloth before hemming and mounting.
Priced and sold by the dozen.   We do not break dozen packages.

DECORATED BROOKLYN FELTS.

Pattern Nos. 09526, 09527 and 13526, 13527.

No.	Decoration.				Color of Shade.	Length.	Per doz
09526	Maroon flock and flitter mixed				Medium drab.	6 feet	$3.30
09527	"	"	"	"	" "	7 "	3.54
13526	"	"	"	"	Light Spanish olive.	6 "	3.30
13527	"	"	"	"	" " "	7 "	3.54

Pattern Nos. 17546 and 17547.

No.	Decoration.				Color of Shade.	Length.	Per doz.
17546	Maroon flock and flitter mixed				Spanish Olive.	6 feet	$3.30
17547	"	"	"	"	" "	7 "	3.54

SEE PERFORATED SLIP AND FRONT PAGES FOR DISCOUNT AND TERMS.

DECORATED MOUNTED WINDOW SHADES.—Continued.
DECORATED BROOKLYN FELTS.—Continued.

Pattern Nos. 03506 and 03507.

No.	Decoration.	Color of Shade.	Length.	Per doz.
03506	Gold bronze	Olive green	6 feet	$3.30
03507	" "		7 "	3.54

Pattern Nos. 12586 and 12587.

No.	Decoration.	Color of Shade.	Length.	Per doz.
12586	Gold bronze	Dark Spanish Olive	6 feet	$3.30
12587	" "		7 "	3.54

Pattern Nos. 07516 and 07517.

No.	Decoration.	Color of Shade.	Length.	Per doz.
07516	Maroon Flock and Glitter mixed	Pea Green.	6 feet	$3.30
07517	" "	" "	7 "	3.54

DECORATED MOUNTED WINDOW SHADES. — Continued.

DECORATED GLAZED HOLLANDS.

PATTERN Nos. S106 and S107.

No.	Decoration,	Color of Shade,	Length,	Per doz.
S106	Olive Flock and Flitter mixed.	Slate,	6ft.	$6.00
S107	" " " " "	"	7ft.	6 70

PATTERN Nos. G116 and G117.

No.	Decoration,	Color of shade,	Length,	Per doz.
G116	Gold Bronze.	Dark Green.	6ft.	$6.00
G117	" "	" "	7ft.	6.70

SEE PERFORATED SLIP AND FRONT PAGES FOR DISCOUNT AND TERMS.

DECORATED MOUNTED WINDOW SHADES.—Continued.

* DECORATED GLAZED HOLLANDS.—Continued.

PATTERN Nos. E126 and E127.

No.	Decoration,	Color of Shade,	Length,	Per doz.
E126	Maroon Flock and Filter Mixed.	Ecru.	6ft.	$6.00
E127	" " " " "	"	7ft.	6 70

PATTERN Nos. D136 and D137.

No.	Decoration,	Color of Shade,	Length,	Per doz.
D136	Maroon Flock and Flitter Mixed.	Drab.	6ft.	$6.00
D137	" " " " "	"	7ft.	6.70

SEE PERFORATED SLIP AND FRONT PAGES FOR DISCOUNT AND TERMS.

DECORATED MOUNTED WINDOW SHADES.—Continued

DECORATED GLAZED HOLLANDS.—Continued.

PATTERN Nos. O156 and O157.

No.	Decoration,	Color of Shade,	Length,	Per doz.
0156	Maroon Flock and Flitter Mixed.	Spanish Olive.	6ft.	$6 00
0157	" " " " "	" "	7ft.	6.70

PATTERN Nos. N176 and N177.

No.	Decoration,	Color of Shade,	Length,	Per doz.
N176	Maroon Flack and Flitter Mixed.	Nile Green.	6ft.	$6 00
N177	" " " " "	" "	7ft.	6.70

SEE PERFORATED SLIP AND FRONT PAGES FOR DISCOUNT AND TERMS.

DECORATED MOUNTED WINDOW SHADES.—Continued.

DECORATED CAYUGAS (NEW) IN ONE EFFECT.

An "Oil Painted" Material. Cloth body; Fibre filled.

Pattern Nos. 03576, 03577 and 09576, 09577.

No.	Decoration.	Color of Shade.	Length.	Per doz.
03576	Gold Bronze..	...Olive Green.	6 feet	$5.30
03577	" "	" "	7 "	5.90
09576	Olive flock and flitter mixed...........................	Medium Drab.	6 "	5.30
09577	" " " "	" "	7 "	5.90

Pattern Nos. 07586, 07587 and 12586, 12587

No.	Decoration.	Color of Shade.	Length.	Per doz.
07586	Maroon flock and flitter mixed............................	Pea Green.	6 feet	$5.30
07587	" " " "	" "	7 "	5.90
12586	White flock..	Dark Spanish Olive.	6 "	5.30
12587	" "	" " "	7 "	5.90

SEE PERFORATED SLIP AND FRONT PAGES FOR DISCOUNT AND TERMS.

DECORATED MOUNTED WINDOW SHADES.—Continued.

DECORATED CAYUGAS IN TWO EFFECTS.

Pattern Nos. 07596, 07597 and 13596, 13597.

No.	Decoration.	Color of Shade.	Length.	Per doz.
07596	Leaves Gold Bronze, veins and twigs Maroon flock	Pea Green.	6 feet	$5.80
07597	" " " " " " "	" "	7 "	6.40
13596	" " " " " Green "	Light Spanish Olive.	6 "	5.80
13597	" " " " " " "	" " "	7 "	6.40

Pattern Nos. 09606, 09607 and 10606, 10607.

No.	Decoration.	Color of Shade.	Length.	Per doz.
09606	Ground work Gold Bronze, lines and tracery White flock	Medium Drab.	6 feet	$5.80
09607	" " " " " " " "	" "	7 "	6.40
10606	" " " " ' " Maroon "	Naples Tint.	6 "	5.80
10607	" " " " " " " "	" "	7 "	6.40

SEE PERFORATED SLIP AND FRONT PAGES FOR DISCOUNT AND TERMS.

DECORATED MOUNTED WINDOW SHADES.—Continued.

DECORATED ONTARIOS IN ONE EFFECT.

Pattern Nos. 01616, 01617 and 05616, 05617.

No.	Decoration.				Color of Shade.	Length.	Per doz.
01616	Maroon flock and flitter mixed				Light blue.	6 feet	$6.00
01617	"	"	"	"	" "	7 "	6.70
05616	Olive	"	"	"	Medium stone.	6 "	6.00
05617	"	"	"	"	" "	7 "	6.70

Pattern Nos. 03626, 03627 and 12626, 12627.

No.	Decoration.				Color of Shade.	Length.	Per doz.
03626	Gold bronze				Olive green.	6 feet	$6.00
03627	"	"			" "	7 "	6.70
12626	Olive flock and flitter mixed				Dark Spanish olive.	6 "	6.00
12627	"	"	"	"	" " "	7 "	6.70

SEE PERFORATED SLIP AND FRONT PAGES FOR DISCOUNT AND TERMS.

DECORATED MOUNTED WINDOW SHADES.—Continued.

DECORATED ONTARIOS IN ONE EFFECT.—Continued.

Pattern Nos. 09636, 09637 and 10636, 10637.

No.	Decoration.	Color of Shade.	Length.	Per doz.
9636	White flock	Medium Drab,	6 feet	$6.00
9637	" "	" "	7 "	6.70
9636	Maroon flock and flitter mixed	Naples Tint,	6 "	6.00
9637	" " " " "	" "	7 "	6.70

DECORATED ONTARIOS IN TWO EFFECTS.

Pattern Nos. 04646 and 04647.

No.	Decoration.	Color of Shade.	Length.	Per doz.
4646	Centres of figures and lower border Gold Bronze, soft lines and tracery Maroon flock	Terra Cotta	6 feet	$6.50
4647	" " " " " " " " " " "	" "	7 "	7.20

DECORATED MOUNTED WINDOW SHADES.—Continued.

DECORATED ONTARIOS IN TWO EFFECTS.—Continued.

PATTERN Nos. 07656, 07657 and 13656, 13657.

No.	Decoration,	Color of Shade,	Length,	I er doz.,
07656	Borders and light lines, gold bronze, Scroll and heavy lines maroon flock,	Pea Green.	6ft.,	$6.50
07657	" " " " " " " " " " " " "	" "	7ft.,	7 20
13656	" " " " " " " " " " " Green Flock,	Light Spanish Olive,	6ft.,	6.50
13657	" " " " " " " " " " " "	" " "	7ft.,	7.20

PATTERN Nos. 14666 and 14667.

No.	Decoration,	Color of Shade, Ecru.	Length,	Per doz.,
14666	Body of Design, Gold Bronze, with soft lines alternating in Gold and Maroon,		6ft.,	$6 50
14667	" " " " " " " " " " " "		7ft.,	7 20

SEE PERFORATED SLIP AND FRONT PAGES FOR DISCOUNT AND TERMS.

DECORATED MOUNTED WINDOW SHADES.—Continued.

DECORATED ONTARIOS. LACE EFFECTS, NO FRINGE.

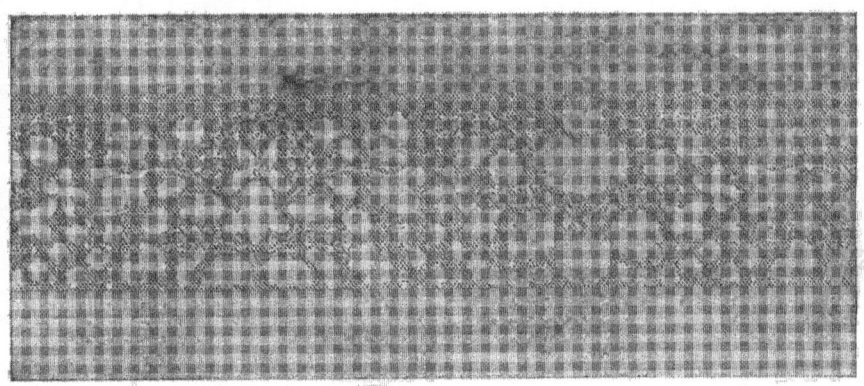

Pattern Nos. 07676, 07677 and 09676, 09677.

No.	Decoration.					Color of Shade.	Length.	Per Doz.
07676	Back Ground in Black Net Work, Lace Effects in White Mica					Pea Green.	6 feet	$7.20
07677	"	"	"	"	"	"	7 "	7.90
09676	"	"	"	"	"	Medium Drab.	6 "	7.20
09677	"	"			"	"	7 "	7·90

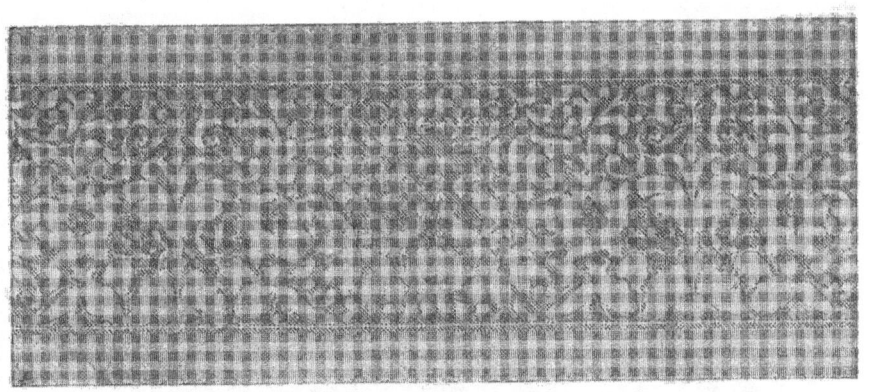

Pattern Nos. 10686, 10687 and 14686, 14687.

No.	Decoration.					Color of Shade.	Length.	Per Doz.
10686	Back Ground in Black Net Work, Lace Effects in White Mica					Naples Tint.	6 feet	$7.20
10687	"	"	"	"	"	"	7 "	7.90
14686	"	"	"	"	"	Ecru.	6 "	7.20
14687	"	"	"	"	"	"	7 "	7.90

SEE PERFORATED SLIP AND FRONT PAGES FOR DISCOUNT AND TERMS.

DECORATED MOUNTED WINDOW SHADES.—Continued.

DECORATED ONTARIOS, LACE EFFECT.—Continued.

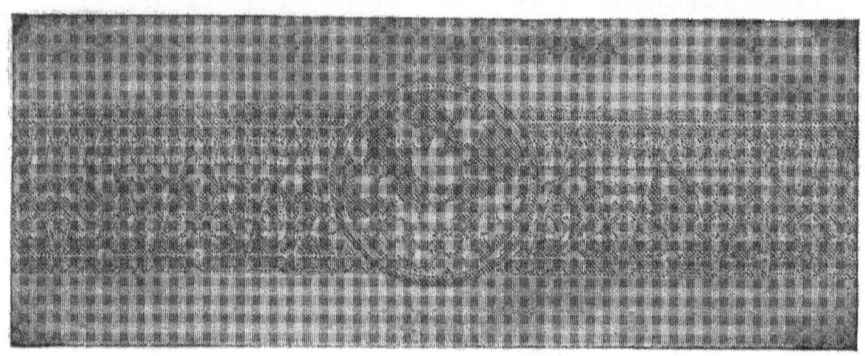

PATTERN Nos. 12696, 12697 and 13696, 13697.

No.	Decoration,	Color of Shade,	Length,	Per doz.,
12696	Background in Black Net Work, Lace Effect in White Mica,	Dark Spanish Olive,	6ft.,	$7.20
12697	" " " " " " " " " "	" " "	7ft.,	7.90
13696	" " " " " " " " " "	Light Spanish Olive,	6ft.,	7.20
13697	" " " " " " " " " "	" " "	7ft.,	7 90

DECORATED SENECAS IN ONE EFFECT.

PATTERN Nos. 03706 and 03707.

No.	Decoration,	Color of Shade,	Length,	Per doz.,
03706	White Flock,	Olive Green,	6ft.,	$7.20
03707	" "	" "	7ft.,	8.20

SEE PERFORATED SLIP AND FRONT PAGES FOR DISCOUNT AND TERMS.

DECORATED MOUNTED WINDOW SHADES.—Continued.

DECORATED SENECAS IN ONE EFFECT.—Continued.

PATTERN Nos. 05716 and 05717.

No.	Decoration,	Color of Shade,	Length,	Per doz.,
05716	Maroon Flock and Flitter Mixed,	Medium Stone,	6ft.,	$7.20
05717	" " " " "	" "	7ft.,	8.20

PATTERN Nos. 07726, 07727 and 10726, 10727.

No.	Decoration,	Color of Shade,	Length,	Per doz.,
07726	Maroon Flock and Flitter Mixed,	Pea Green,	6ft.,	$7.20
07727	" " " " "	" "	7ft.,	8.20
10726	" " " " "	Naples Tint,	6ft.,	7.20
10727	" " " " "	" "	7ft.,	8.20

SEE PERFORATED SLIP AND FRONT PAGES FOR DISCOUNT AND TERMS.

DECORATED MOUNTED WINDOW SHADES.—Continued.

DECORATED SENECAS IN ONE EFFECT.—Continued.

PATTERN Nos. 09736 and 09737.

No.	Decoration,	Color of Shade,	Length,	Per doz.,
09736	Olive Flock and Flitter Mixed,	Medium Drab,	6ft ,	$7.20
09737	" " " " "	" "	7ft ,	8 20

PATTERN Nos. 12746 and 12747.

No.	Decoration,	Color of Shade,	Length,	Per doz.,
12746	Gold Bronze,	Dark Spanish Olive,	6ft.,	$7.20
12747	" "	" " "	7ft.,	8.20

SEE PERFORATED SLIP AND FRONT PAGES FOR DISCOUNT AND TERMS.

DECORATED MOUNTED WINDOW SHADES,—Continued.

DECORATED SENECAS IN TWO EFFECTS.

Pattern Nos. 07756, 07757 and 10756, 10757.

No.	Decoration.	Color of Shade.	Length.	Per doz.
07756	Body of design Gold Bronze, outlines and shadings White flock	Pea Green.	6 feet	$7.80
07757	" " " " " " " "	" "	7 "	8.80
10756	" " " " " " Green "	Naples Tint.	6 "	7.80
10757	" " " " " " " "	" "	7 "	8.80

Pattern Nos. 09766, 09767 and 12766, 12767.

No.	Decoration.	Color of Shade.	Length.	Per doz.
09766	Body of design Gold Bronze, with outlines in Silver Metallics	Medium Drab.	6 feet	$7.80
09767	" " " " " " " "	" "	7 "	8.80
12766	" " " " " " " "	Dark Spanish Olive.	6 "	7.80
12767	" " " " " " " "	" "	7 "	8.80

SEE PERFORATED SLIP AND FRONT PAGES FOR DISCOUNT AND TERMS.

DECORATED MOUNTED WINDOW SHADES.—Continued.

DECORATED SENECAS IN THREE EFFECTS.

Pattern Nos. 13776, 13777.

No.	Decoration.	Color of Shade.	Length.	Per Doz.
13776	Green flock and irridescent flitter on gold bronze................Light Spanish Olive.		6 feet	$8.20
13777	" " " " " .... " " "		7 "	9.20

DECORATED SENECAS IN FIVE EFFECTS.

Pattern Nos. 07836, 07837 and 12826, 12827.

No.	Decoration.	Color of Shade.	Length	Per Doz.
07836	Gold, copper and light blue bronzes, Maroon flocks, silver metallics........ ......Pea Green.		6 feet	$9.50
07837	" " " " " " .... " "		7 "	10.50
12826	" " " " " "	Dark Spanish Olive.	6 "	9.50
12827	" " " " " "	" " "	7 "	10.50

SEE PERFORATED SLIP AND FRONT PAGES FOR DISCOUNT AND TERMS.

DECORATED MOUNTED WINDOW SHADES.—Continued.
DECORATED SENECAS IN FIVE EFFECTS.—Continued.

Pattern Nos. 13836, 13837 and 14836, 14837.

No.	Decoration.	Color of Shade.	Length.	Per doz.
13836	Gold, Blue and Purple Bronzes, Maroon flock, Silver Metallics......Light Spanish Olive		6 feet	$9.50
13837	" " " " " " " " " " "		7 "	10.50
14836	" " " " " " " " ....Ecru.		6 "	9.50
14837	" " " " " " " " .... "		7 "	10.50

DECORATED MINETTOS IN TWO EFFECTS.

Pattern Nos. 08796, 08797 and 16796, 16797.

No.	Decoration.	Color of Shade.	Length.	Per doz.
08796	Design in Irridescent flitter, with stencil in Copper...........................Fawn.		6 feet	$8.20
08797	" " " " " " .... "		7 "	9.40
16796	" " " " " " ....Salmon.		6 "	8.20
16797	" " " " " " .... "		7 "	9.40

DECORATED MOUNTED WINDOW SHADES.—Continued.

DECORATED MINETTOS IN THREE EFFECTS.

PATTERN Nos. 05806, 05807 and 09806, 09807.

No.	Decoration,	Color of Shade,	Length	Per doz.
05806	Maroon Flock and Irredescent Flitter on Gold Bronze,	Medium Stone,	6ft.	$ 8.80
05807	" " " " " " " "	" "	7ft.	10.00
09806	White " " " " " " "	" Drab,	6ft.	8.80
09807	" " " " " " " "	" "	7th	10.00

DECORATED MINETTOS IN FIVE EFFECTS.

PATTERN Nos. 07816, 07817 and 10816, 10817.

No.	Decoration,	Color of Shade,	Length,	Per doz.
07816	Gold, Copper and Green Bronzes, Bronze and Silver Metallics,	Pea Green,	6ft.	$ 9.60
07817	" " " " " " " " "	" "	7ft,	10.80
10816	" " " " " " " " "	Naples Tint,	6ft.	9.60
10817	" " " " " " " " "	" "	7ft,	10.80

SEE PERFORATED SLIP AND FRONT PAGES FOR DISCOUNT AND TERMS.

DECORATED MOUNTED WINDOW SHADES.—Continued.

LACE EFFECTS WITH FRINGES ON "ONTARIO" CLOTH WITH COMBINATION FRINGE IN WHITE AND
COLOR OF SHADE, ALTERNATING. A NOVEL EFFECT.

PATTERN Nos. 02846, 02847 and 14846, 14847.

No.	Decoration,									Color of Shade,	Length,	Per doz.,
02846	Design in White Mica, with Imitation Meshes, White Fringe,							"	"	White,	6ft.,	$ 9.50
02847	"	"	"	"	"	"	"	"	"	"	7ft.,	10.20
14846	"	"	"	"	"	"	"	Combination Ecru Fringe,		Ecru,	6ft.,	9.50
14847	"	"	"	"	"	"	"	"	"	"	7ft.,	10.20

PATTERN Nos. 12856, 12857 and 13856, 13857.

No.	Decoration,									Color of Shade,	Length,	Per doz.,
12856	Design in White Mica, with Imitation Meshes, Combination Fringe,							"	"	Dark Spanish Olive,	6ft.,	$ 9.50
12857	"	"	"	"	"	"	"	"	"	"	"	"	7ft.,	10.20
13856	"	"	"	"	"	"	"	"	"	Light	"	"	6ft.,	9.50
13857	"	"	"	"	"	"	"	"	"	"	"	"	7ft.,	10.20

SEE PERFORATED SLIP AND FRONT PAGES FOR DISCOUNT AND TERMS.

OUR SHADE MANUFACTURING DEPARTMENT.

WE make a specialty of manufacturing shades in special sizes for residences, stores, and office buildings. We use only *the best* materials and employ skilled workmen, and guarantee the shades we turn out first-class in every respect. Estimates furnished.

For the benefit of our customers we submit herewith illustrations showing the different methods of hanging shades, and giving instructions for the proper measurement of windows.

All measurements for the width should be made from point to point on each side of casing where brackets are to be placed.

All measurements for the length of shade should be the net measurement from top to bottom of window.

We will make the necessary allowances in width for the satisfactory working of shade, and in length for the hem and turn upon roller when shade is drawn down full length.

When shades are to be hung, as illustrated in Fig. 1, on the outside or surface of casing facing the room, give exact distance from points as designated by *W* to *X*, being extreme distance from point to point where brackets are to be placed, and for length of shade the distance from *M* to *N*, and state in ordering, "outside bracket measure."

The shades when finished will be from 1 to 1½ inches narrower than your measurement, and contain 6 inches more of cloth.

When shades are to be hung, as illustrated in Fig. 2, on the inside or surface of the casing which face each other, give the distance from *J* to *Z*, the exact distance from jamb to jamb of window at points where brackets will be fastened, and for length the distance from *Q* to *R*, and state in ordering, "inside bracket measure."

Measurements for shades hung in this manner should be very accurate, even to a sixteenth of an inch.

Measure each window separately.

State whether shades are to roll from top or bottom of window. In the former the roller is fastened at the top, and in the latter case at the bottom of window.

In hanging shades observe carefully the printed instructions on each roller regarding the proper adjustment of spring.

USE ONLY THE "EFFICIENT" FIXTURES.

SEE PERFORATED SLIP AND FRONT PAGES FOR DISCOUNT AND TERMS.

OUR SHADE MANUFACTURING DEPARTMENT.

W E make a specialty of this department of our business, and guarantee the shades which we turn out the best which first-class material and skilled workmanship can produce.

Below we give a schedule of prices for making up shades in various sizes. In ascertaining costs of shades from this schedule, it will be necessary to use the prices for dimensions next larger than the shades you desire, unless the shades wanted are exactly the same as schedule dimensions. *For instance*, a shade 66 inches wide and 9 feet 6 inches long, will cost the price given for a shade 72 inches wide and 10 feet long.

We use only the well-known "Efficient" spring stop roller in our special order work, and mount all shades of this nature on rollers of sufficient size and strength to perform the work required in a satisfactory manner.

SCHEDULE OF PRICES FOR SHADES IN SPECIAL SIZES.

Made from "Onondaga" Hand-Made Opaque, mounted upon "Efficient" spring stop rollers—ready to hang.
Sizes in schedule are for shades when finished.   Prices are for single shades.

LENGTH OF SHADE FINISHED.	WIDTH OF SHADE IN INCHES.									
	37	42	45	48	54	63	72	81	90	104
4 feet	.74	.88	1.10	1.52	1.68	2.30	2.72	3.24	3.66	4.20
5 "	.86	1.00	1.20	1.68	1.88	2.50	3.00	3.52	4.00	4.60
6 "	.94	1.14	1.40	1.80	2.06	2.70	3.20	3.82	4.40	5.00
7 "	1.04	1.28	1.56	2.00	2.24	2.90	3.50	4.10	4.72	5.40
8 "	1.12	1.42	1.68	2.16	2.42	3.10	3.80	4.38	5.08	5.80
9 "	1.34	1.62	1.84	2.38	2.62	3.30	4.20	5.00	5.44	6.20
10 "	1.42	1.84	2.00	2.48	3.00	3.50	4.60	5.30	6.00	6.80
11 "	1.52	2.00	2.14	2.64	3.20	3.70	5.10	5.60	6.50	7.40
12 "	1.60	2.16	2.50	2.80	3.70	3.93	5.50	5.90	7.00	8.00
13 "	1.90	2.50	2.72	3.20	4.20	4.50	5.90	6.20	7.40	8.60
14 "	2.00	2.70	2.92	3.36	4.40	4.70	6.30	6.50	7.80	9.20
15 "	2.10	2.90	3.12	3.52	4.60	4.90	6.70	7.00	8.20	10.00

Lettering, in plain shaded gold letters, 50c. per lineal foot.

Special Note.—In ordering state whether the measurements given are *cloth* or *bracket* measure, and if bracket whether *inside* or *outside*; see illustration and explanation on previous page. State color of cloth desired; if shades are wanted 48 inches wide or wider, much correspondence and annoyance will be saved if selection of color is made in "Onondaga" goods only, as our other brands of opaque shadings are not manufactured in all widths, and the matching of their colorings in hand-made goods is not at all satisfactory. If any lettering is wanted, inclose a printed card bearing name or names to be used. We cannot be responsible for misspelling where shades are lettered in other than the English language.

See page 30 for list of "Onondaga" colorings. *Sample books mailed on application.* Special colorings will have to be made to order at an extra expense, and the time necessary to make the cloth will be from ten days to two weeks.

See next page for cost of finishing any of above shades with fringes.
See pages 33-39 for cuts and description of fringes.

SCHEDULE OF PRICES OF BANCROFT'S "SUN FAST" HOLLAND SHADES, IN SPECIAL SIZES.

Mounted ready to hang.   Prices are for single shades.

LENGTH OF SHADE FINISHED.	WIDTH OF SHADE IN INCHES.							
	36	40	42	44	48	54	60	72
4 feet	.90	1.00	1.10	1.30	1.70	2.00	2.20	3.00
5 "	1.10	1.20	1.30	1.40	1.90	2.30	2.40	3.30
6 "	1.20	1.30	1.40	1.60	2.20	2.50	2.70	3.70
7 "	1.30	1.50	1.70	1.80	2.40	2.80	3.00	4.00
8 "	1.60	1.70	1.80	2.00	2.60	3.00	3.30	4.40
9 "	1.70	1.90	2.00	2.20	2.80	3.30	3.60	4.80
10 "	1.90	2.00	2.20	2.40	3.10	3.50	3.90	5.20
11 "	2.00	2.20	2.30	2.60	3.30	3.80	4.20	5.50
12 "	2.20	2.40	2.50	2.80	3.50	4.00	4.50	5.90

We can finish any of the above Shades with fringe upon the bottom as per prices below, which are for fringe and labor only, and to be added to the cost of plain Shade.

STYLE OF FRINGE.	WIDTH OF SHADE IN INCHES.							
	36	40	42	44	48	54	60	72
No. 480	.08	.10	.12	.13	.14	.16	.18	.20
" 64	.18	.20	.22	.24	.26	.28	.30	.32
" 425	.22	.24	.26	.28	.30	.32	.34	.36
" 600	.30	.34	.36	.38	.40	.42	.44	.46
" 550	.36	.40	.42	.46	.50	.60	.70	.80
" 2070	.36	.40	.42	.46	.50	.60	.70	.80
" 1000	.44	.50	.56	.62	.68	.74	.82	.92
" 2000	.50	.60	.70	.80	.90	1.00	1.10	1.20
" 2071	.50	.60	.70	.80	.90	1.00	1.10	1.20

See pages 33 to 39 for cuts and descriptions of fringes.

BANCROFT'S "SUN FAST" HOLLANDS.

THESE GOODS ARE GUARANTEED NOT TO FADE.

WIDTHS.	30 in.	34 in.	36 in.	42 in.	48 in.	54 in.	60 in.	72 in.
White	.29	.31	.32	.42	.54	.62	.70	.90
Colors	.31	.33	.34	.44	.56	.64	.74	.94
Extra for cutting	.06	.06	.06	.06	.10	.10	.10	.10

Send for sample book of colors.

JOHN KING & SON'S SCOTCH HOLLANDS.

WIDTHS.	28 in.	32 in.	36 in.	42 in.	48 in.	54 in.	60 in.	72 in.
White	.26	.30	.34	.40	.48	.58	.66	.82
Cream and Ecru	.30	.34	.38	.44	.54	.64	.72	.90
No. 30 Sage	.32	.36	.40	.48	.58	.70	.78	.94
" 40 "	.34	.38	.42	.50	.62	.74	.86	1.02
Green	.38	.42	.46	.54	.66	.76	.86	1.06
Blue	.38	.42	.46	.54	.66	.76	.86	1.06
Extra for cutting	.06	.06	.06	.08	.10	.12	.16	.20

SEE PERFORATED SLIP AND FRONT PAGES FOR DISCOUNT AND TERMS.

"EFFICIENT" WOOD ROLLERS.

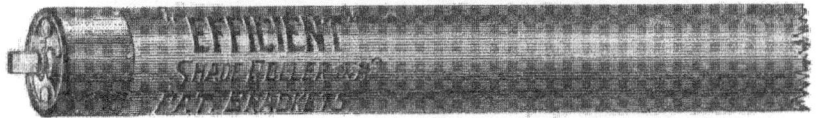

WE ARE AGENTS, AND GUARANTEE THEM THE BEST.

ORDER BY NUMBER.   NO CHARGE FOR PACKING OR CARTAGE.   F. O. B. NEW YORK.

No.	Diameter.	Length.	Packed.	Ends.		Per Gross.
100	1 inch,	42 inches,	1 Gross,	Iron,	....	$27.00
102	1 "	42 "	½ "	"	....	27.00
104	1 "	42 "	⅓ "	"	....	27.00
120	1 "	42 "	1 "	Brass Caps	....	28.00
122	1 "	42 "	1½ "	"	....	28.00
124	1 "	42 "	⅓ "	"	....	28.00
190	Extra Brass Caps for 1 inch Rollers				..............................per gross,	1.50
192	" Outside Brackets "				..............................per doz. sets,	20
194	" Inside " "				............................." "	20
200	1¼ inch,	42 inches,	1 Gross,	Iron,	....	41.00
202	1¼ "	42 "	½ "	"	....	41.00
204	1¼ "	42 "	¾ "	"	....	41.00
224	1¼ "	42 "	¼ "	Brass Caps	....	42.50
250	1¼ "	48 "	1 "	Iron,	....	42.00
252	1¼ "	48 "	½ "	"	....	42.00
254	1¼ "	48 "	¼ "	"	....	42.00
274	1¼ "	48 "	¼ "	Brass Caps	....'....	43.50
300	1¼ "	54 "	1 "	Iron,	....	54.00
302	1¼ "	54 "	1½ "	"	....	54.00
304	1¼ "	54 "	¼ "	"	....:.....	54.00
350	1¼ "	60 "	1 "	"	....	64.00
352	1¼ "	60 "	1½ "	"	....	64.00
354	1¼ "	60 "	¼ "	"	....	64.00
390	Extra Brass Caps for 1¼ inch Rollers				..............................per gross,	2.00
392	" Outside Brackets				..............................per doz. sets,	20
394	" Inside " "				............................." "	20

Patent Brackets will be packed with any of above when so ordered, without extra charge.

" PEOPLE'S " WOOD ROLLERS.

No.	Diameter.	Length.	Packed.	Bracket.	Ends.		Per Gross.
500	15-16 inch,	42 inches,	1 Gross,	Regular,	Iron,	....	$18.00
502	15-16 "	42 "	1½ "	"	"	....	18.00
510	15-16 "	42 "	1 "	"	Brass Caps	....	19.00
512	15-16 "	42 "	½ "	"	"	....	19.00
590	Extra Brass Caps for 15-16 inch Rollers					..............................per gross,	1.50
592	" Brackets " " "					..............................per doz. sets,	20

" VERMONT " WOOD ROLLERS.

No.	Diameter.	Length.	Packed.	Ends.		Per Gross.
600	1⅜ inch,	42 inches,	1 Gross,	Iron,	....	$35.00
602	1⅜ "	42 "	½ "	"	....	35.00
604	1⅜ "	42 "	¼ "	"	....	35.00
610	1⅜ "	48 "	1 "	"	....	36.00
612	1⅜ "	48 "	½ "	"	....	36.00
614	1⅜ "	48 "	¼ "	"	....	36.00
688	Extra Brass Caps for 1⅜ inch Rollers				....	2.00
690	" Nickel " " "				....	3.00

SLATS.

5 feet long, 1¼ inches wide	..............per doz. $0.70		10 feet long, 2 inches wide	..............per doz. $3.20
6 " " 1¼ " "	.... " 80		11 " " 2 " "	.... " 3.60
7 " " 1½ " "	.... " 96		12 " " 2 " "	.... " 3.84
8 " " 1½ " "	.... " 1.20		13 " " 2½ " "	.... " 6 40
9 " " 1½ " "	.... " 1.50		14 " " 2½ " "	.... " 7.00

SEE PERFORATED SLIP AND FRONT PAGES FOR DISCOUNT AND TERMS.

"EFFICIENT" TIN ROLLERS.

1⅛-INCH DIAMETER.

Made up to 5 feet long, and suitable for shades 12 feet long, in assorted lengths.

	Each.
2 feet 2 inches long and under....................	$0.48
2 feet 4 inches to 4 feet........................	58
Over 4 feet long................................	72
Extra Brackets for 1⅛-inch Tin Roller, per doz. sets	30

1½-INCH DIAMETER.

Made from 2 feet to 6 feet long, and suitable for shades 12 feet long.

4 feet long and under........................	$0.72
4 feet 2 inches to 5 feet.	96
Over 5 feet long..............................	1.20
Extra Brackets for 1½-inch Tin Roller, per doz. sets	80

1¾-INCH DIAMETER.

Made from 2 feet to 9 feet, and suitable for shades up to 12 feet long.

4 feet and under	$1.20
4 " 2 inches to 5 feet	1.34
5 " 2 " 6 "	1.44
6 " 2 " 7 "	1.56
7 " 2 " 8 "	1.68
Over 8 feet.................................	1.80
Extra Brackets for 1¾-inch Tin Roller, per doz. sets	1.00

2¼-INCH DIAMETER.

Made from 5 feet to any required length; for heavy shades.

6 feet and over, per foot........................	$0.48

3¼-INCH DIAMETER.

Made from 7 feet to any required length; for extra long and heavy shades, maps and awnings.

7 feet and over, per foot........................	$0.84

4-INCH DIAMETER.

Made from 12 feet to any required length; for very wide and heavy shades, maps and awnings.

12 feet long and over, per foot..................	$1.80

An allowance of 25 cents per case, net ($1.00 a gross), is made on 1⅛-inch Rollers when packed in quarter gross cases—36 of one diameter in a case.

An allowance of 50 cents per case, net ($2.00 a gross), is made on 1½ and 1¾-inch Rollers when packed in quarter gross cases—36 of one diameter in a case.

Ordering in regular packing is not only economy, but damage in shipment is prevented by the uniformity of sizes in the same box. With a little care you can make your order so as to obtain the deduction.

NEW

PATENT

"EFFICIENT"

SHADE

FIXTURE

BRACKET.

Is the most important improvement in shade rollers since 1867. It is at once an inside, outside, top, bottom, ceiling and car bracket. It works equally well either side up, can be used like an ordinary bracket by those who do not believe in new things, and the roller will work in any bracket that may have been in use. Under all conditions the pawls may be made to engage or not by merely changing the roller end for end.

THE "EFFICIENT" WOOD AND TIN SPRING STOP FIXTURES.

—ALSO—

THE "VERMONT" AND "PEOPLE'S" ROLLERS.

Manufactured by NEVIUS & HAVILAND, VERGENNES, VT.,

ARE THE BEST MADE. WE CARRY A COMPLETE STOCK. SATISFACTION GUARANTEED.

SEE PERFORATED SLIP AND FRONT PAGES FOR DISCOUNT AND TERMS.

MINETTO OPAQUE SHADE CLOTH.
MACHINE-MADE.
NOT MADE ABOVE 45 INCHES WIDE.

		Per Yard	
		In full pieces.	When cut.
38 inches wide, about 60 yards in piece.	$0.25		$0.27
42 " " "		42 } 20%	41
45 " " 60 " "		48 } disc.	46

WE CARRY IN STOCK.

No.	Color.	No.	Color.
4	Marine Blue.	38	Light Pea Green.
5	Electric Blue.	50	Tan.
9	White.	52	Fawn.
10	Emerald Green.	54	Mushroom.
14	Dark Olive.	56	Medium Drab.
15	Olive Green.	58	Naples Tint.
16	Olive Bronze.	60	Old Gold.
17	Pea Green.	62	Light Gold.
18	Sage.	64	Dark Spanish Olive.
19	Light Olive Bronze.	65	Medium Spanish Olive.
20	Seal Brown.	66	Light Spanish Olive
22	Chestnut Brown.	68	Ecru.
26	Terra Cotta.	70	Copper.
30	Slate.	72	Dark Salmon.
32	Medium Stone.	74	Salmon.
34	Dark Slate.	75	Dark Pea Green.

Sample books furnished upon application.

ONONDAGA OPAQUE SHADE CLOTH.
HAND-MADE.
THE AVERAGE LENGTH OF A PIECE IS 45 YARDS.

	Per Yard	
	In full pieces.	When cut.
37 inches wide	$0.25	$0.27
42 " "	37	41
45 " "	42	46
48 " "	50	60
54 " "	57	68
63 " "	66	80
72 " "	75	90
81 " "	90	1.08
90 " "	1.04	1.26
104 " "	1.28	1.53

WE CARRY IN STOCK.

No.	Color.	No.	Color.
600	Crylight Green.	654	Olive.
604	Golden Brown.	655	Stone.
617	Light Blue.	656	Fawn.
630	Ivory White.	661	Olive Yellow.
638	Pea Green.	663	Cream.
640	Light Olive.	664	Blue.
641	Medium Drab.	666	Spanish Olive.
643	Light Drab.	667	Flesh Tint.
644	Pure Drab.	669	Light Spanish Olive.
649	Light Quaker Drab.	680	Old Gold.
650	Light Gold.	681	Yellow Drab.
652	Light Fawn.	702	Terra Cotta.

We carry in stock all the above in all widths, except
Nos. 630, 641, 643, 650, 656, 680, which we have from 37
inches to 72 inches.
Sample books furnished upon application.

"ONTARIO" WATER COLORED OPAQUE
MADE 36 INCHES WIDE ONLY—ABOUT 60 YARDS IN PIECE.

No.	Color	No.	Color
205	Light Blue.	256	Medium Drab.
215	Olive Green.	258	Naples Tint.
226	Terra Cotta.	264	Light Olive.
232	Medium Stone.	266	Spanish Olive.
238	Pea Green.	268	Ecru.

Per yard...................$0.16
We do not cut full pieces.

"CRITERION" AMERICAN GLAZED HOLLAND.
MADE 36 INCHES WIDE ONLY IN A FULL PIECE.
The above we carry in ecru, blue, Spanish olive,
slate, brown, green, Nile green.......per yard, $0.15
We do not cut full pieces.

SENECA OIL OPAQUE.
MADE 36 INCHES WIDE ONLY—60 YARDS IN A PIECE.

No.	Color.	No.	Color
105	Light Blue.	156	Medium Drab.
115	Olive Green.	158	Naples Tint.
126	Terra Cotta.	164	Light Olive.
132	Medium Stone.	166	Spanish.
138	Pea Green.	168	Ecru.

Per yard....................$0.22
We do not cut full pieces.

PAPER WINDOW SHADES.

Plain	green, brown, stone, blue,	per roll of 8 yards	$0.40
Figured	green, brown, olive, stone, buff, blue,	per roll of 5 curtains...	50

COTTON BALL CORD.
PACKED ONE DOZEN OF A COLOR IN A BOX.

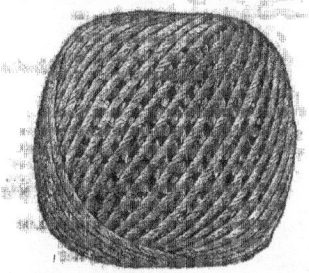

Per dozen balls.......................$0.72
We carry in stock all colors to match "Minetto" goods.

WINDOW LINE CORD.
HALF GROSS IN A PIECE.

Per gross yards $0.72
Ecru, green, scarlet, blue, brown, light olive, olive
and stone.

BRAIDED TRAVERSE CORD.
FOR STORE SHADES.
72 YARDS ON A CARD—2 CARDS IN A BOX.

We carry in blue, brown, ecru, light olive, olive,
stone......................per gross yards, $2.30

SEE PERFORATED SLIP AND FRONT PAGES FOR DISCOUNT AND TERMS.

NASH'S ADJUSTABLE SHADE BRACKET.

INDISPENSABLE TO HEALTH AND COMFORT.

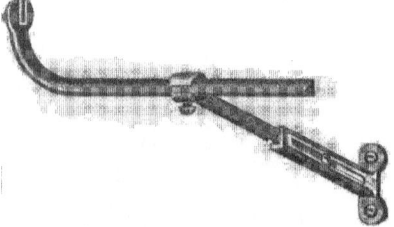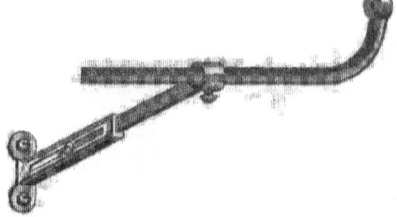

Showing Left Hand Bracket.   **Showing Right Hand Bracket.**

The Adjustable Shade Bracket is a new invention. It is so formed as to fit any depth window jamb and extend out over the casing. By using this bracket the shade is attached to the upper window sash instead of the casing, but allowing it to occupy the same extended position on the casing as with the old style fixtures.

The result is that in lowering the upper sash to admit fresh air or to allow the foul air to escape, the shade is also lowered, allowing the air to pass freely in and out above it, which gives perfect ventilation without the constant whipping and rattling of the shade by the wind.

Perfect ventilation from top can be secured, while the shade can cover the lower part of the window.

No. 25   Adjustable to any ordinary window (no roller)..............per dozen pairs, $3.70 ; per gross pairs, $42.00

"EFFICIENT," "VERMONT" AND "PEOPLE'S" ROLLERS CAN BE USED IN THESE BRACKETS.

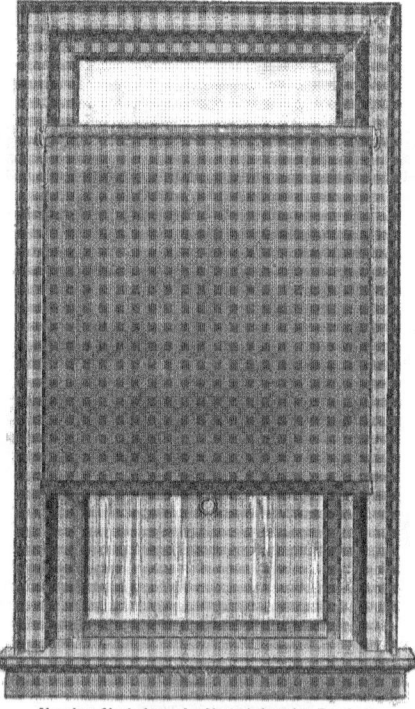

Showing window with Bracket on upper sash, with Shade Roller.   Showing Shade hung by Nash Adjustable Brackets.

SEE PERFORATED SLIP AND FRONT PAGES FOR DISCOUNT AND TERMS.

LAKESIDE WINDOW SHADE GUIDE.

An attachment to run the shade straight, and prevent damaging the cloth. Of invaluable use in hotels, schools and large apartment buildings.

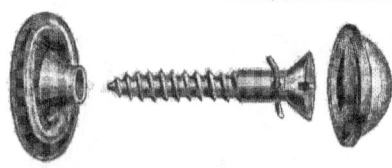

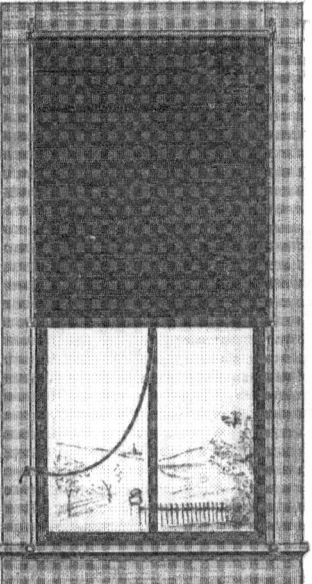

It consists of an L-shaped piece of steel with screw to put up under bracket to hold the wire, 8 feet of copper wire, a screw with perforated head to tighten the wire, with an adjustable porcelain head and a steel detachable device for the end of the slat which runs up and down on the wire. Cuts illustrate the different parts and the complete guide as it is attached to the shade and window frame.

The different parts are packed complete with wire in neat paper box. One dozen sets in a carton.

No.	Per Doz.
10	$2.00

ROSE ADJUSTABLE SHADE EXHIBITOR.

For use on side wall or ceiling.   Adjustable to any width shade.

Cut shows Exhibitor as used on Ceiling.

No.		Each.
605	Made of ash, adjustable; capacity 24 shades	$2.00

SEE PERFORATED SLIP AND FRONT PAGES FOR DISCOUNT AND TERMS.

WYANT'S PATENT SHADE FASTENERS.

For fastening shades on the roller in a neat manner without the use of tacks.

No.						Per Gross.
A	1¼ inches long, for 15-16 and 1 in. roller......					$1.50
B	1¼	"	"	1⅛	" 1¼ "	..... 1.50

"NATIONAL" SHADE CLINCHER.

Made from best Bessemer steel. Quickly adjusted. Never wears out. Requires but three clinchers to 3 foot shade. Costs little more than tacks. Cheapest fastener on the market.
No. 10 for 1 in. and 1¼ in. rollers, per gross...... $1.00

Pat. Feb. 22, 1887.

IRON WIRE NAILS.

No.						Per Pkge
13	⅞ inch, one pound in package........					$0.11
13	1	"	"	"	"	10
13	1¼	"	"	"	"	10

MOULDING NAILS.

No.						
14	1½ inch, one pound in package........					10
14	2	"	"	"	"	9

SHADE TACKS.

	Doz. Papers.
1 oz., Swedes, Iron...........................	$0.30

WOOD SCREWS.

6

SUITABLE FOR CURTAIN FIXTURES.

Packed one gross in a box.

No.		Per Gross.
6	⅝ inch, Iron	$0.20
06	⅝ " Brass, for pole brackets.......	48

UPRIGHT PULLEYS.

No.		Per Doz.
10	⅝ in., Bronze...........................	$0.80

SIDE PULLEYS.

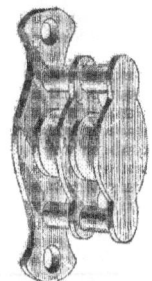 

No. 100.   No. 60.

No.		Per Doz.
60	Bronzed Iron, fancy......................	$0.74
100	Brass, double, plain..................	2.00

PALMER'S STOP PULLEYS.

No.		Per Gross.
1	Screw	$7.00

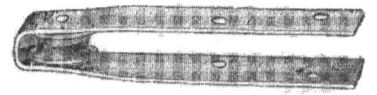

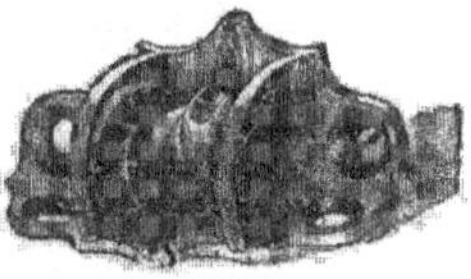

No.		Per Gross.
12	Shade...................................	$7.00

SLAT PULLEY.

No.		Per Doz.
35	⅝ inch, Brass...........................	$.90

BRASS SCREW PULLEYS.

No.		Per Doz.
20	Full size cut, ⅝ inch......................	$1.00
30	Same pulley, 1 "	2.30

SEE PERFORATED SLIP AND FRONT PAGES FOR DISCOUNT AND TERMS.

SHADE FRINGES.

26 yards on a card, except Nos. 480 and 64, which contain 72 yards each.   We also quote prices at which we will finish 36 inch shades with the different fringes.   Price of cloth extra.

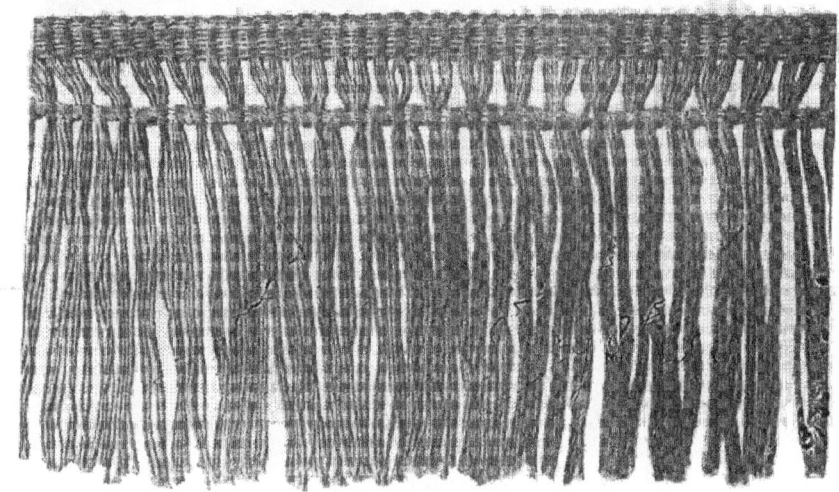

No. 480   Imitation Linen. 3½ inches..,......Per Gro. Yards. $5.80
      For Fringe and labor on 1 doz. 3 foot Shades..   .80
        In stock in Minetto colors 4, 5, 14, 16, 17, 20, 26, 30, 34, 54, 60, 64, 66, 74.

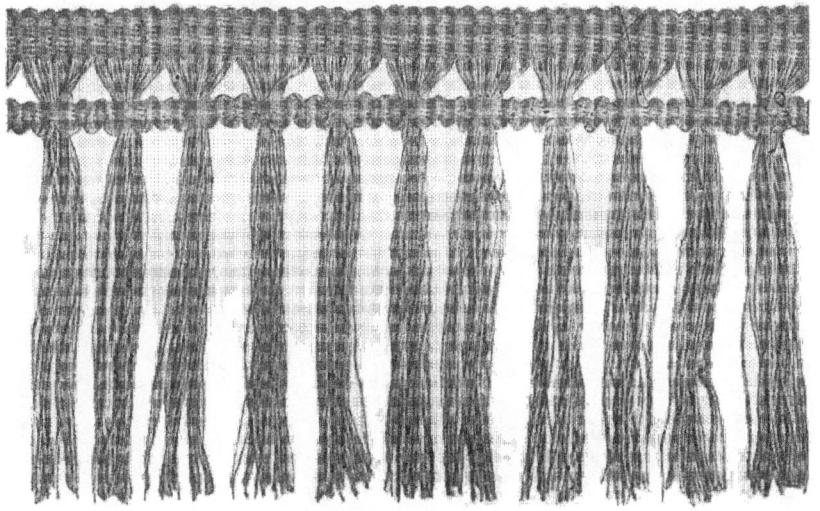

No. 64   Glazed Cotton, 4 inches...Per Gro. Yards. $11.40
      For Fringe and labor on 1 doz. 3 foot Shades...   1.60
        In stock in Minetto colors 5, 9, 15, 17, 26, 34, 54, 56, 58, 60, 64, 66, 68, 74.

SEE PERFORATED SLIP AND FRONT PAGES FOR DISCOUNT AND TERMS.

SHADE FRINGES—Continued.

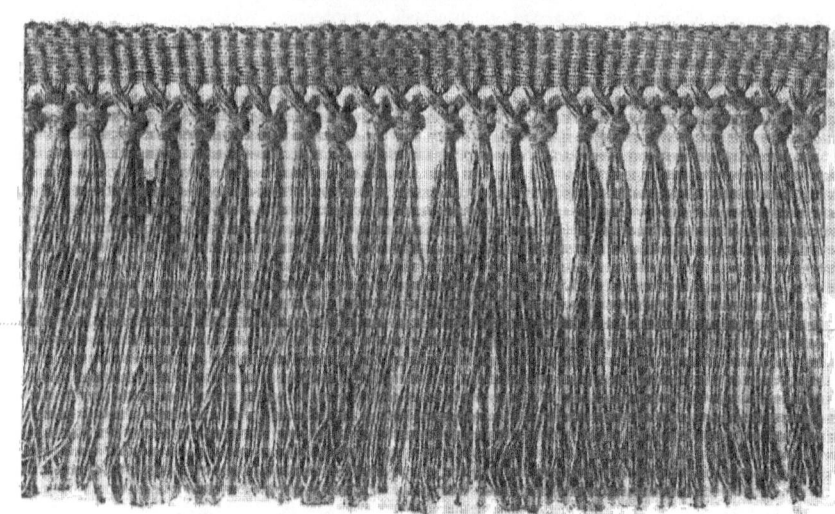

No.
425   Glazed Cotton, 4½ inches..   Per Doz. Yards.
....$1.20
For Fringe and labor on 1 doz. 3 foot Shades.. 2.20
In stock in Minetto colors 5, 15, 16, 26, 32, 54, 56, 60, 64, 68, 74.

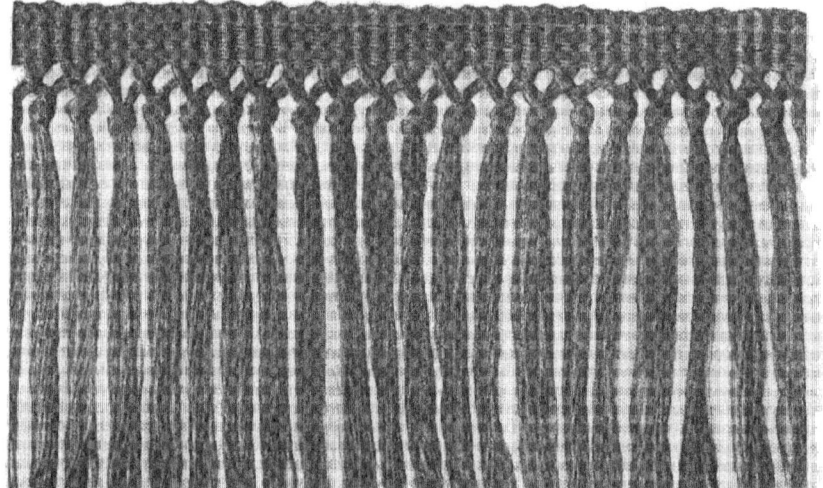

No.
600   Linen, Single Knot, 5 inches...   Per Doz. Yards.
....$2.20
For Fringe and labor on 1 doz. 3 foot Shades.. 2.70
In stock in Minetto colors 9, 14, 16, 17, 20, 26, 34, 54, 60, 64, 66, 68, 74.   Also Onondaga colors 643, 644, 652, 656, 680.

SEE PERFORATED SLIP AND FRONT PAGES FOR DISCOUNT AND TERMS.

SHADE FRINGES.—Continued.

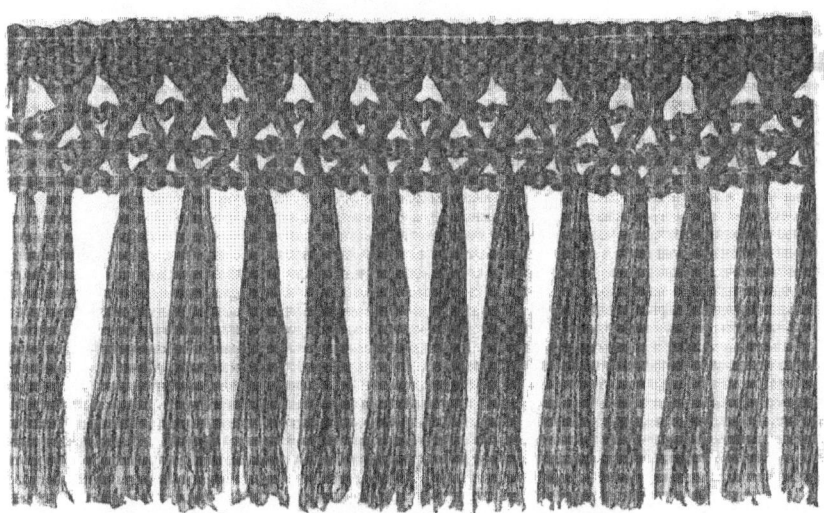

No.
2070   Linen, 5¼ inches.. Per Doz. Yards. $3.40
          For Fringe and labor on 1 doz. 3 foot Shades.................................... 3.00
              In stock in Minetto colors, 5, 9, 15, 17, 26, 34, 54, 56, 58, 64, 66, 68, 74.

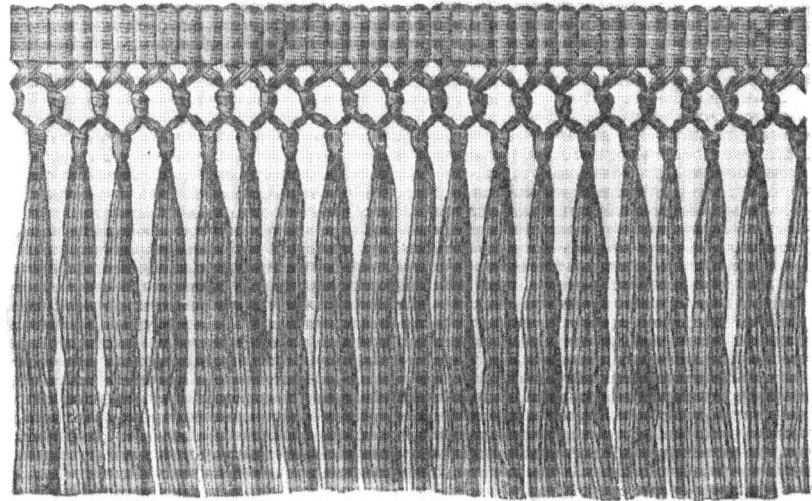

No.
550   Linen, Double Knot, 5 inches.. Per Doz. Yards. $2.70
          For Fringe and labor on 1 doz. 3 foot Shades.................................. 3.20
              Stock in Minetto colors, 5, 9, 16, 17, 26, 34, 54, 64, 66, 68, 74.

SEE PERFORATED SLIP AND FRONT PAGES FOR DISCOUNT AND TERMS.

SHADE FRINGES—Continued.

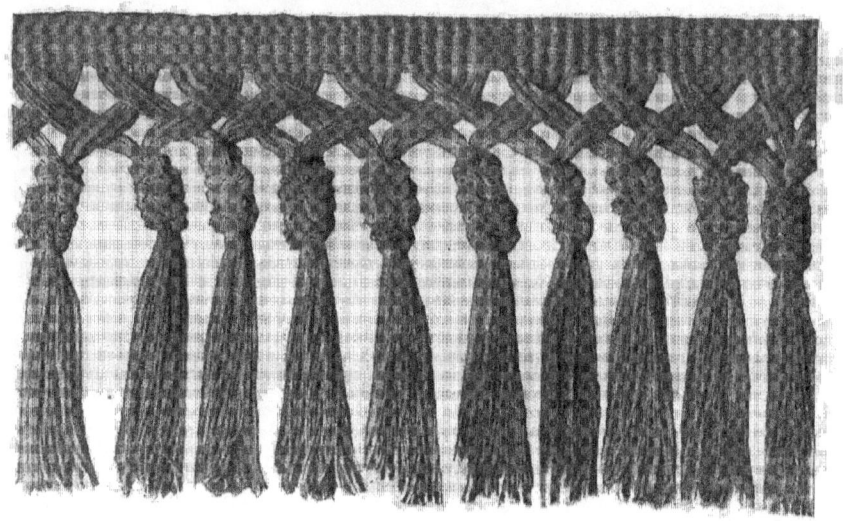

No.
1000 Linen, Fancy Tassel, 5½ inches... ....$3.40
 For Fringe and labor on 1 doz. 3 foot Shades......... .... 4.30

In stock in Minetto colors 9, 14, 16, 17, 20, 26, 34, 54, 60, 64, 66, 68, 74.

Per Doz. Yards.

No.
2000 Linen, Fancy Head, 4½ inches............ .. ..$4.00
 For Fringe and labor on 1 doz. 3 foot Shades... 4.60

Per Doz. Yards.

In stock in Minetto colors 9, 14, 16, 17, 26, 64, 66, 68, 74.

Also Onondaga colors 643, 644, 652, 656, 680.

SEE PERFORATED SLIP AND FRONT PAGES FOR DISCOUNT AND TERMS.

SHADE FRINGES—Continued.

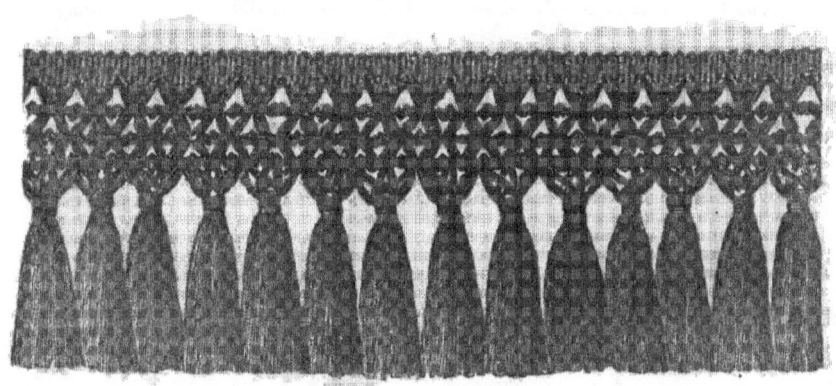

No.   Per Doz. Yards.
2071 Linen, Fancy Head, 5 inches... $4.20
      For Fringe and labor on 1 doz. 3 foot Shades.................................... 4.80

In stock in Minetto colors, 9, 15, 32, 38, 64, 68.

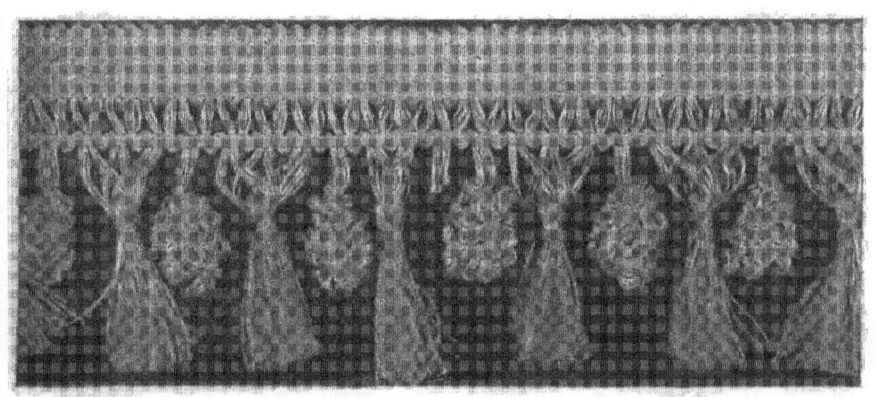

No.   Per Doz. Yards.
"M" Linen, Fancy Tassel, 3½ inches...$5.50
     For Fringe and labor on 1 doz. 3 foot shade............................... 6.00

In stock in Minetto colors, 5, 15, 32, 38, 56, 58, 64, 66.

SEE PERFORATED SLIP AND FRONT PAGES FOR DISCOUNT AND TERMS.

SHADE PULLS.

All Numbers on this page are packed ¼ gross, with Clasps, in box.

Note.—All our ring shade pulls, except 413 and 423, are made of Brass tubing, either polished or nickelplated, and are very much superior to cast iron goods merely washed over, which soon wear black. All with McGill fasteners.

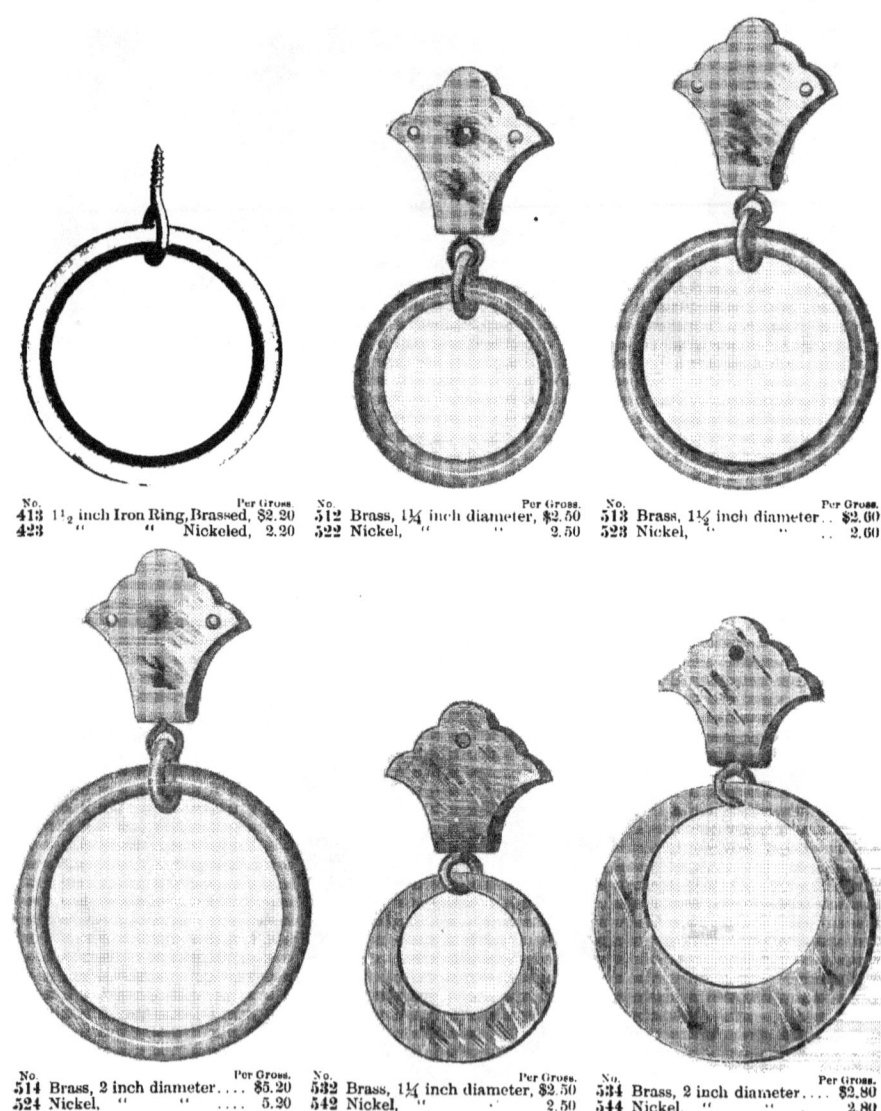

No.		Per Gross.
413	1½ inch Iron Ring, Brassed,	$2.20
423	" " " Nickeled,	2.20

No.		Per Gross.
512	Brass, 1¼ inch diameter,	$2.50
522	Nickel, " "	2.50

No.		Per Gross.
513	Brass, 1¼ inch diameter..	$2.60
523	Nickel, " " ..	2.60

No.		Per Gross.
514	Brass, 2 inch diameter....	$5.20
524	Nickel. " "	5.20

No.		Per Gross.
532	Brass, 1¼ inch diameter,	$2.50
542	Nickel, " "	2.50

No.		Per Gross.
534	Brass, 2 inch diameter....	$2.80
544	Nickel. " "	2.80

SEE PERFORATED SLIP AND FRONT PAGES FOR DISCOUNT AND TERMS.

SHADE PULLS.—Continued.

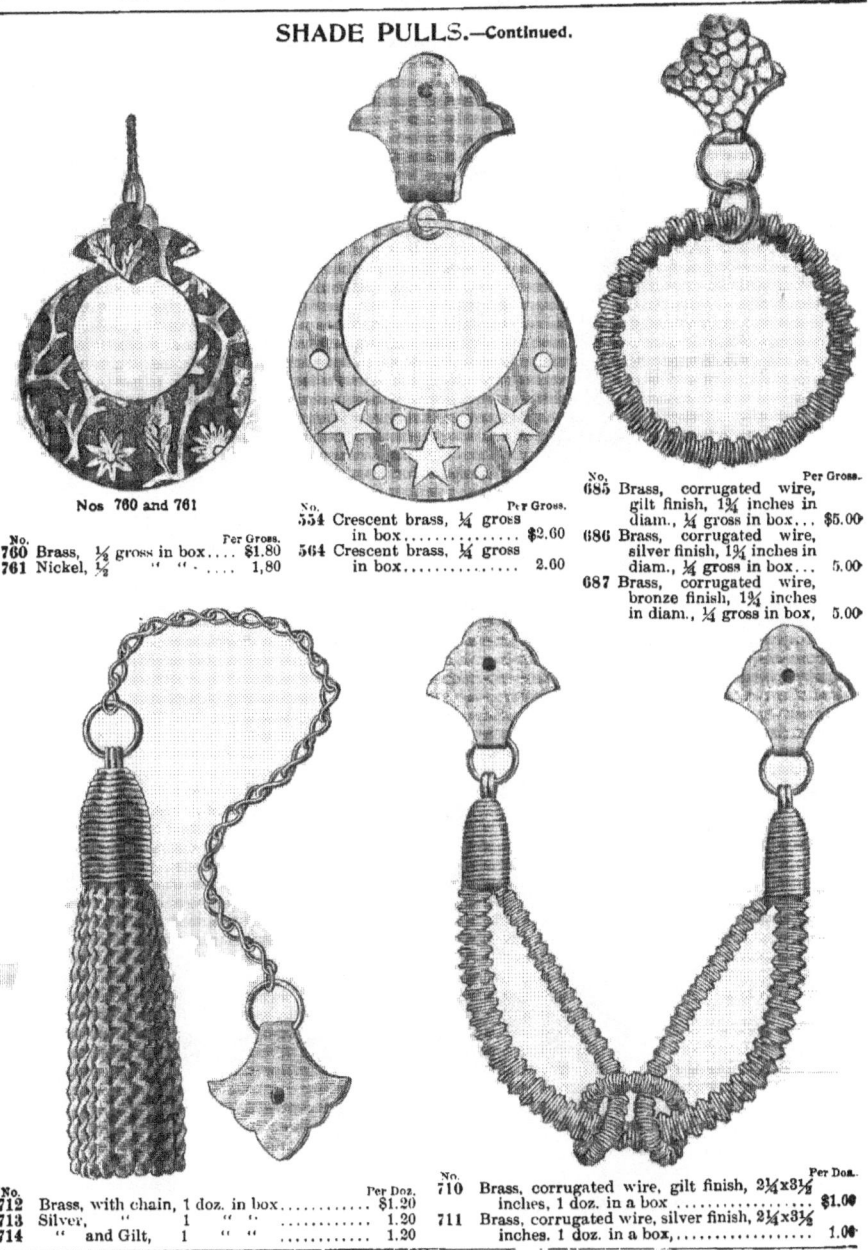

Nos 760 and 761

No.		Per Gross.
760	Brass, ½ gross in box....	$1.80
761	Nickel, ½ " "	1.80

No.		Per Gross.
554	Crescent brass, ¼ gross in box..............	$2.60
564	Crescent brass, ¼ gross in box..............	2.60

No.		Per Gross.
685	Brass, corrugated wire, gilt finish, 1¾ inches in diam., ¼ gross in box..	$5.00
686	Brass, corrugated wire, silver finish, 1¾ inches in diam., ¼ gross in box...	5.00
687	Brass, corrugated wire, bronze finish, 1¾ inches in diam., ¼ gross in box,	5.00

No.		Per Doz.
712	Brass, with chain, 1 doz. in box...........	$1.20
713	Silver, " 1 " "	1.20
714	" and Gilt, 1 " "	1.20

No.		Per Doz.
710	Brass, corrugated wire, gilt finish, 2¼x3½ inches, 1 doz. in a box	$1.00
711	Brass, corrugated wire, silver finish, 2¼x3½ inches. 1 doz. in a box,.................	1.00

SEE PERFORATED SLIP AND FRONT PAGES FOR DISCOUNT AND TERMS.

SHADE PULLS.—Continued.

All Numbers on this page packed one dozen in a box.

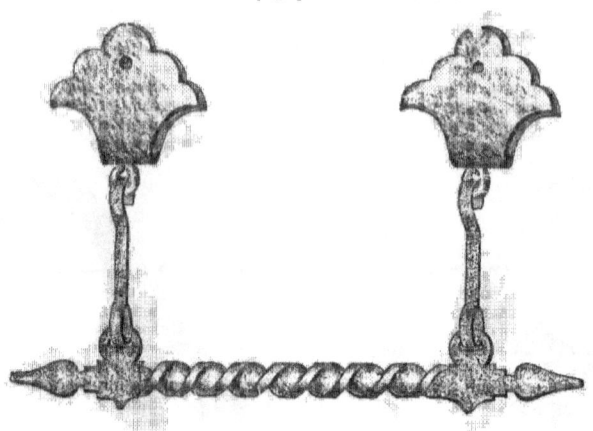

No.		Per Doz.
630	4½ inch Brass....	$0.60
631	4¼ " Nickel	60

No.		Per Doz.
632	Brass	$0.70
633	Silver	70
634	Olive and Silver	70

SEE PERFORATED SLIP AND FRONT PAGES FOR DISCOUNT AND TERMS.

SHADE PULLS.—Continued.

CORRUGATED AND SPIRAL WIRE SHADE PULLS.

No.		Per Doz.
705	Brass, gilt finish, 3x3½ inches, 1 doz. in a box	$0.90
706	" silver " 3x3½ " 1 " "	90

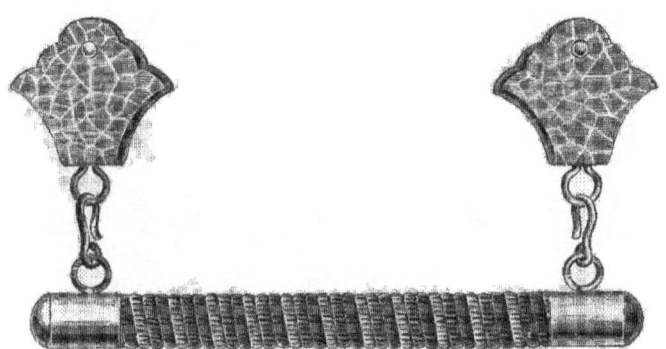

The ferrules or tips of this pull are nickelplated, highly polished; the chains and clasps are silverplated.

No.		Per Doz.
680	4 inch, Heliotrope and Silver Spiral Wire, nickel ends, 1 doz. in a box	$1.10
681	4 " Silver and Gold Spiral Wire, nickel ends, 1 doz. in a box	1.10

SEE PERFORATED SLIP AND FRONT PAGES FOR DISCOUNT AND TERMS.

SHADE PULLS.—Continued.
SILK BALL AND RING PULLS.
Packed in one-quarter gross boxes.

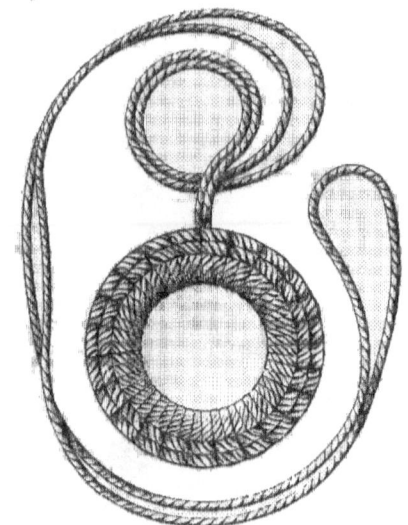

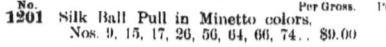

No.		Per Gross.	Per Doz.
1201	Silk Ball Pull in Minetto colors,		
	Nos. 9, 15, 17, 26, 56, 64, 66, 74..	$9.00	$0.90

No.		Per Gross.	Per Doz.
1017	Silk Ring Pull in Minetto colors,		
	Nos. 9, 15, 17, 26, 56, 64, 66, 74..	$9.00	$0.90

NOVELTY PATENT SHADE CORD FASTENER.

Cuts only illustrate manner of fastening cords.   Ordinary ball cord or shade line may be used as well.

A great improvement over screw rings and screw eyes.

No.		Per Gross
4778	Brass, polished, one gross in a box	$5.50

SEE PERFORATED SLIP AND FRONT PAGES FOR DISCOUNT AND TERMS.

SHADE PULLS.—Continued.

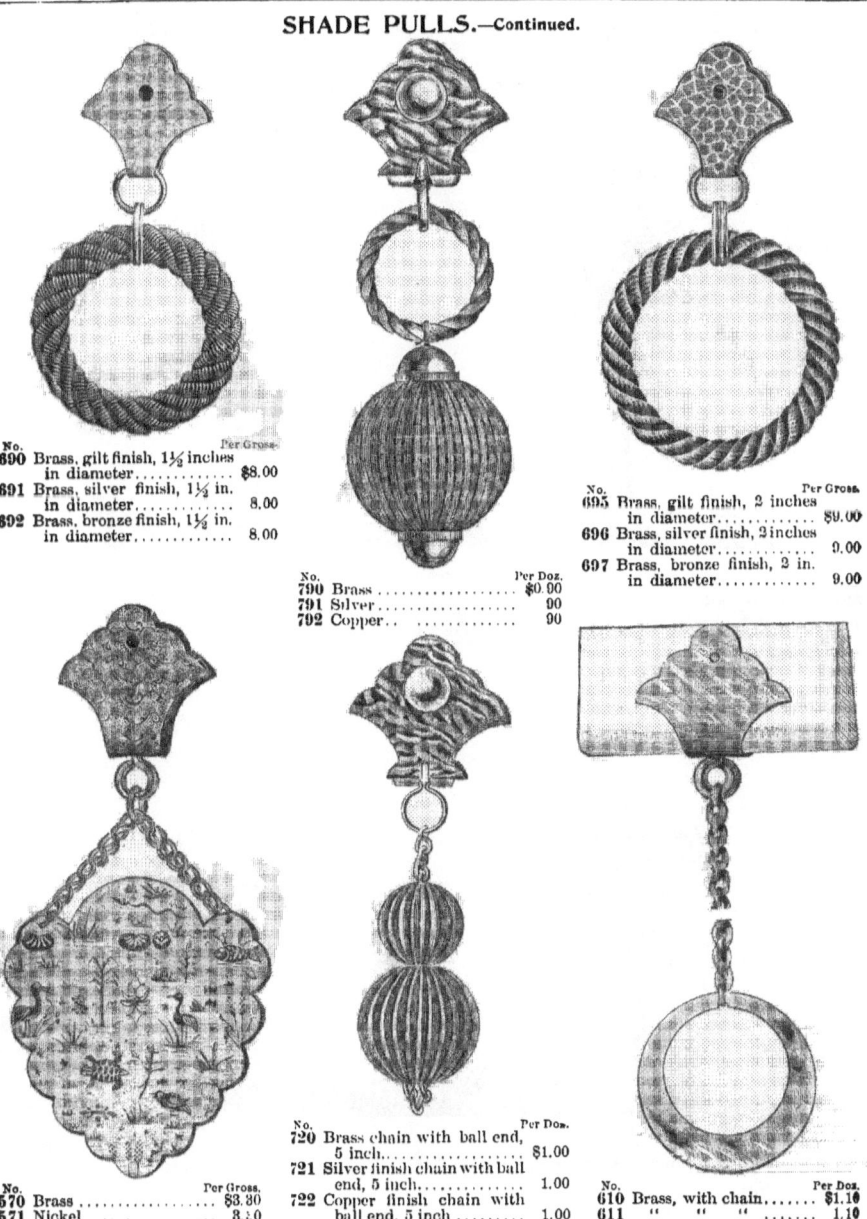

No.		Per Gross.
690	Brass, gilt finish, 1⅝ inches in diameter	$8.00
691	Brass, silver finish, 1⅝ in. in diameter	8.00
692	Brass, bronze finish, 1⅝ in. in diameter	8.00

No.		Per Doz.
790	Brass	$0.00
791	Silver	90
792	Copper	90

No.		Per Gross.
695	Brass, gilt finish, 2 inches in diameter	$9.00
696	Brass, silver finish, 2 inches in diameter	9.00
697	Brass, bronze finish, 2 in. in diameter	9.00

No.		Per Gross.
570	Brass	$3.30
571	Nickel	3.30

No.		Per Doz.
720	Brass chain with ball end, 5 inch	$1.00
721	Silver finish chain with ball end, 5 inch	1.00
722	Copper finish chain with ball end, 5 inch	1.00

No.		Per Doz.
610	Brass, with chain	$1.10
611	" " "	1.10

SHADE PULLS.—Continued.

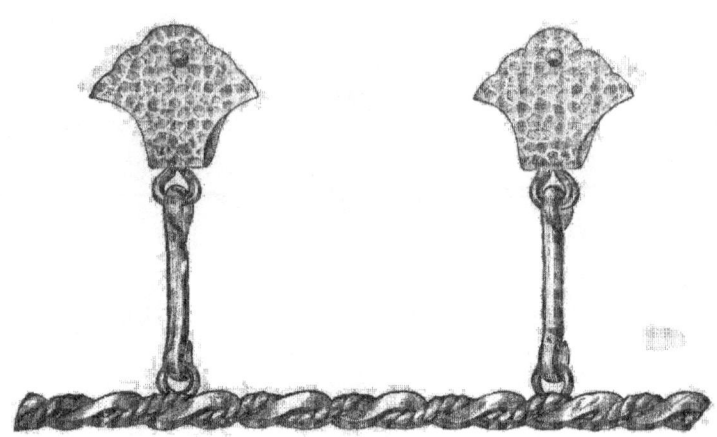

No.								Per Doz.
670	Brass,	4½ inch, with clasps, one doz. in a box						$0.90
671	Silver,	4½ "	"	"	"	"		90
672	Copper,	4½ "	"	"	"	"		90

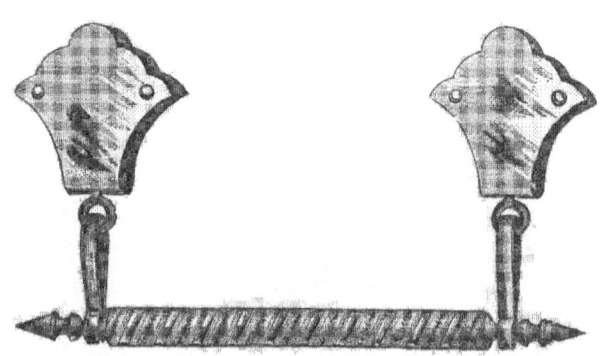

No.							Per Doz.
655	4 inch, Burnished Brass, with clasps, one doz. in a box						$1.00
656	4 " Nickel,	"		"	"	"	1.10

SEE PERFORATED SLIP AND FRONT PAGES FOR DISCOUNT AND TERMS.

SHADE PULLS.—Continued.

No.		Per Doz.
730	Brass, very handsome design, 4¾ inches, one doz. in a box....................................	$1.50
731	Oxidized Silver finish, same as No. 730, " "	1.50

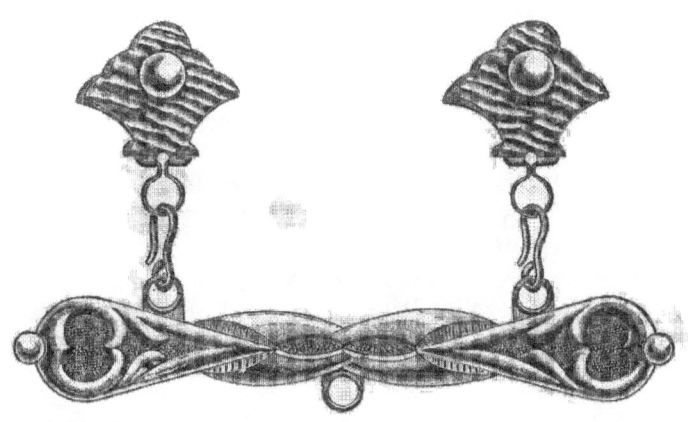

No.		Per Doz.
735	Brass, handsome design, 4¾ inches, one doz. in a box..	$1.50
736	Oxidized Silver finish, same as No. 735, " "	1.50

SEE PERFORATED SLIP AND FRONT PAGES FOR DISCOUNT AND TERMS.

DEVICES FOR USE IN WINDOW SHADE AND WALL PAPER STORES.

THE YEOMAN REVOLVING SHADE EXHIBITOR.

The Exhibitor can be turned around to any point desired, so as to draw out any curtain for inspection. It can be fastened on the side wall, out of the way of other goods, requiring no floor room to show your samples. It is the best device of the kind ever invented for showing curtains full size, and will save its cost the first year selling "remnant" curtains alone, not mentioning convenience of displaying new ones. Each Exhibitor has 24 Spring Fixtures, all fitted and ready to tack on the curtains, or can be furnished without rollers, if preferred.

With Rollers..Each, $15.00
Without Rollers... .... "   10.00

DUNKLE ADJUSTABLE WINDOW SHADE STRIP.

The most complete Shade Hanger in the market. Can be adjusted to suit any width of shade from 34 to 40 inches. Brackets and nails complete with each hanger. Can be retailed at 10 cents each at handsome profit to the dealer. Packed ¼ gross in heavy paper boxes. We do not break boxes.

Price...per Gross, $18.00

SEE PERFORATED SLIP AND FRONT PAGES FOR DISCOUNT AND TERMS.

LAKESIDE BUNDLE HORSES.
FOR COUNTER AND FLOOR USE, IN TYING OR BUNDLING WALL PAPER.

No. 651.

No. 652.

No. **Each.**
651 Small iron revolving horse for counter use; holds 25 rolls.......................... $2.00

No. **Each.**
652 Iron revolving horse for counter use, made of heavy iron with hardwood crossbars, holds 50 rolls............................ $4.00

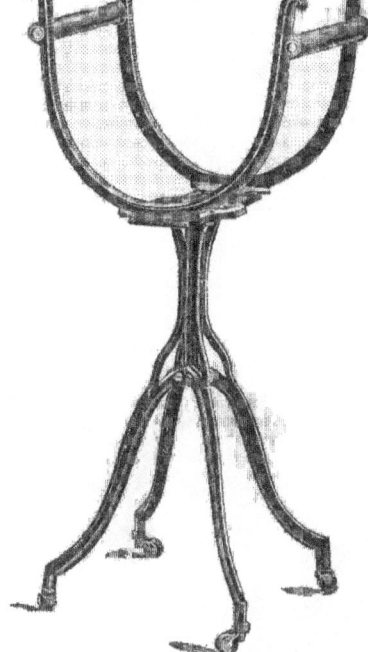

No. 653.

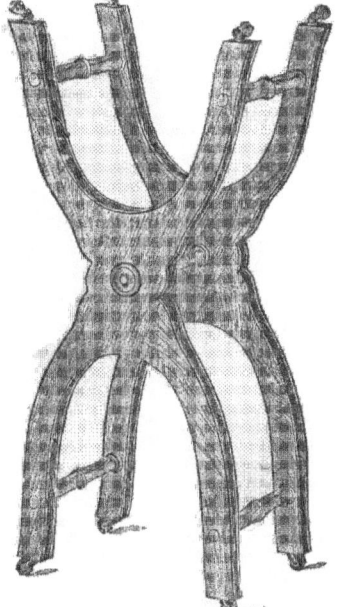

No. 654.

No. **Each.**
653 Large iron; on four iron legs, hardwood crossbars, castors for floor use $6.00

No. **Each.**
654 Reversible; hardwood throughout, oil finish, turned rungs, castors on both ends........ $6.00

SEE PERFORATED SLIP AND FRONT PAGES FOR DISCOUNT AND TERMS.

LAKESIDE BUNDLE HORSE.

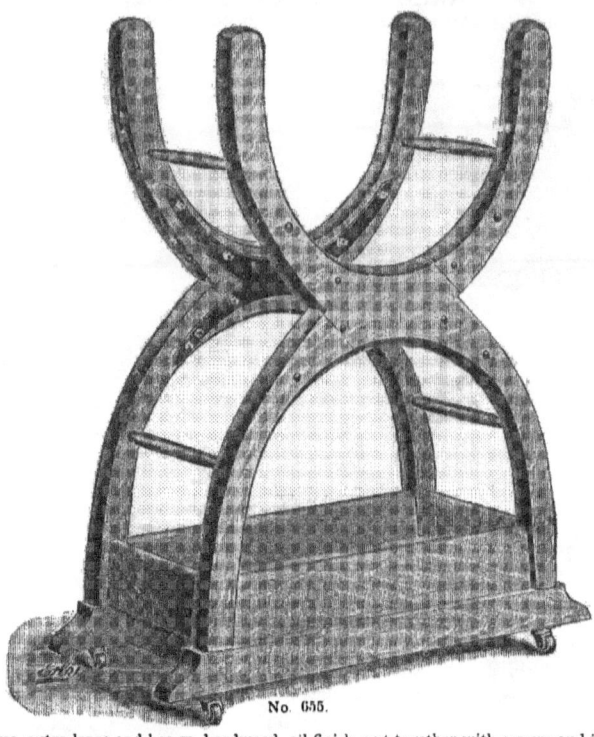

No. 655.

No.		Each.
655	Jobber's Horse, extra large and heavy, hardwood, oil finish, put together with screws and iron braces, large tray in bottom, castors..	$12.00

LAKESIDE WALL PAPER AND BORDER TAGS.

Used by Retail Dealers in sampling and keeping stock of Wall Paper and Borders.

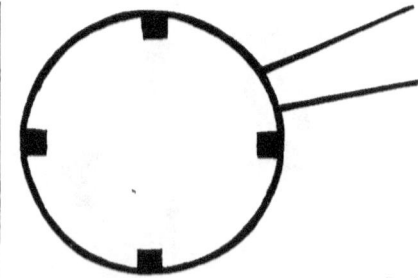

Per 100.

Border Tags; Nos. 1 to 500 packed 50 consecutive numbers in a box; Nos. 501 to 1,000 packed 100 consecutive numbers in a box; each box containing a card of duplicate numbers (*above cut exact size*)................................ $2.00
Extra Duplicate Numbers on cardboard for border disc.. 20
Wall Paper Tags; disc is 2¼ inches in diameter; number pasted flat on tag; numbers range from 1 to 500, in boxes of 50................. 4.00

Per 100.

Jobbers' Tags; same as border tag, except that disc is 1⅝ inches in diameter, containing 12 *plain* labels, which can be removed as they become useless.. $3.00

SEE PERFORATED SLIP AND FRONT PAGES FOR DISCOUNT AND TERMS.

WALL PAPER DISPLAY AND SAMPLE BOOK RACKS.

READING'S WALL PAPER EXHIBITOR.

LITTLE LAKESIDE DISPLAY RACK.

No. 620.

No. 630.

No.		Each.
620	Cherry stained, nicely covered with imitation upholsters' leather	$7.50

No.		Each.
630	Nicely finished in ash, for showing Wall Paper samples on same principle as our No. 610, only on one side	$7.00

THE NATIONAL WALL PAPER RACK AND BINDER.

The first and only PERFECT BINDER made to bind Wall Paper in sample books. A pleasure to show Wall Paper where the National Rack is used. An ornament to any Store.

No.		Each.
650	Rack and Binder complete	$10.00
50	Extra Binders	1,50

SEE PERFORATED SLIP AND FRONT PAGES FOR DISCOUNT AND TERMS.

WALL PAPER DISPLAY RACKS.—Continued.

READING'S "KNOCK-DOWN" WALL PAPER EXHIBITOR WITH SLIDING EXTENSION.

ADJUSTABLE SHELF-PARTITIONS.

No. 625.

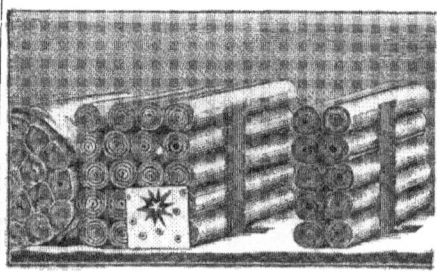

No.
625 Same as No. 620, with sliding extension, for showing combinations.................. $11.00

Each.

No.
662 Made of japanned iron, and take up no shelf room, keep patterns separate, and stock can be condensed as sold, as Partition is movable. Packed 50 in a case.

Per case.......... .... $12.00
Per dozen................................. 4.00

LAKESIDE WALL PAPER DISPLAY RACK.

Will hold four hundred samples thirty-two inches long, two hundred on each side; Cut shows one side closed, samples locked up, raised to a level like a table, and out of the way of dust, etc. The side in operation is held at this angle, or any other desired angle, by a self-acting ratchet as shown by figure 2; The samples are held in place by a self-binding device which a child can

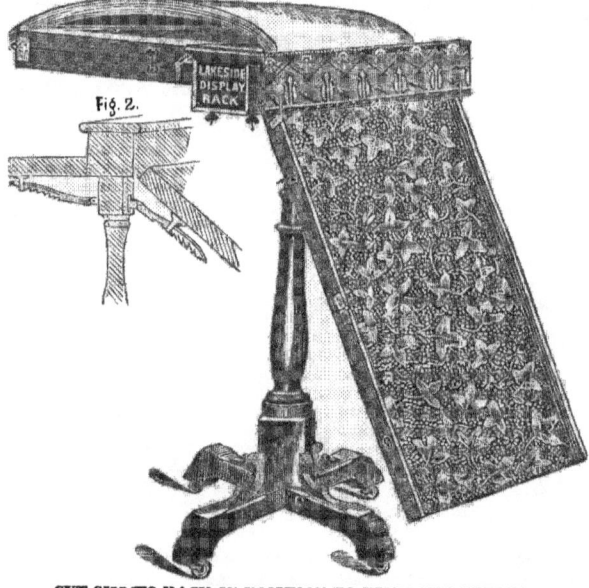

Fig. 2.

understand and operate; no sample book is required as the binder does the work; a device is attached which will hold the border samples in proper place and at proper angle; 50 pieces of cardboard are supplied upon which the various widths of borders can be mounted. Built of hardwood, by skilled labor, and the handsomest Wall Paper Display Rack in the market.

CUT SHOWS RACK IN POSITION TO DISPLAY SAMPLES.

NO. EACH.
610 Rack with Border Cards, complete... 20.00
615 Extra Sets of Cards for Borders... 4.00

SEE PERFORATED SLIP AND FRONT PAGES FOR DISCOUNT AND TERMS.

READING'S TELESCOPIC EXTENSION WALL PAPER EXHIBITOR.

Patented January 5, 1892.

This Exhibitor is intended for showing wall paper in the roll. The special feature is the telescopic extension, by means of which it is instantly lengthened, The display leaf is supplied with a ratchet, so that it may be adjusted to any angle to secure the proper light on the goods.

The Exhibitor is made of oak and white wood finished antique, and provided with castors.

The display leaf is covered with an imitation of upholsterers' leather.

The regular size is four feet high, three feet eight inches long when closed, and six feet long when fully extended.

Special sizes made to order.

No.		Each.
635	44 inches, extends to 72 inches	$32.00

EXHIBITOR PARTLY EXTENDED.

LAKESIDE WALL PAPER SAMPLER.

No.		Per 100.
600	Made of heavy tin; size of surface for showing sample, 4½ inches square. The best device ever offered for sampling wall paper in bins	$8.00

READING'S SAMPLE-BOOK STAND.

No. 660.

The most complete, economical and convenient device in existence for holding and showing sample books.

The cut fully illustrates the stand and the method of hanging and keeping the books when not in use. The display leaf at end is adjustable, and so simple as to need no explanation. The crossbars, upon which the books are hung, are attached to pivoted arms, which swing from side to side and make an opening of sufficient width to allow a book to be easily replaced.

The crossbars should be labeled to correspond with the books which belong to them. By this means any desired book can be quickly found and taken out or put back.

This stand is equally good for wall paper, window shade cloth, table and carriage oil cloth, and all other goods sampled in book form.

It is made of oak, well finished and mounted on castors.

645	Will hold 27 books, 2 ft. x 3 ft.	Each, $30.00

SEE PERFORATED SLIP AND FRONT PAGES FOR DISCOUNT AND TERMS.

WALL PAPER TRIMMERS.
THE READING COMBINED TRIMMER AND MEASURING MACHINE.
Patented March 17, 1891, and May 16, 1893.

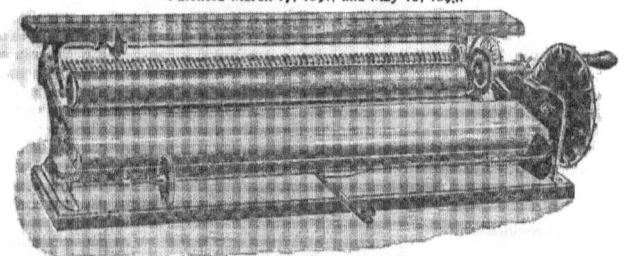

Will trim or measure separately, or do both at the same time. Two of the latest improved winding rods go with each machine. One is for rapid winding, and the other for close or compact winding. The latter makes the rolls as small and tight as when they left the factory.

As a Wall Paper Trimmer it is noiseless, rapid, simple and durable. It is the only Trimmer made without a noisy cog-wheel gear, and trims faster and makes a cleaner cut than any other machine in the market. It trims 22 inch paper, with any width margin up to 2 inches. The knives are made of the best saw steel, carefully tempered, ground and finished, and the whole machine is run by a single endless rubber belt. When the belt becomes slack from any cause, it can be instantly tightened by adjusting a screw provided for that purpose. A metal fender prevents the trimmings from winding into the roll, and conducts them away from the machine.

As a Measuring Machine it is rapid and accurate. Every inch of paper or border is honestly counted, and it never gets "rattled" nor forgets the number of yards measured. It automatically unrolls, accurately measures and compactly re-rolls the paper or border at one operation. It is useful in taking inventory or sorting up and measuring cut rolls and remnants; also for trimming and measuring off a single roll in filling orders.

No.		Each.
606	Combined Machine........	$30.00
602	Trimmer only.........	20.00

ALLEN'S
Keystone Double Trimmer.

ELECTRO-PHOTOTYPE Co PHILA

No.		Each
100	Two sets of cutting knives; trims both edges of the paper at the same time; makes a clean, true cut for butting; will trim either 20 or 22 inch paper; 200 pieces of paper can easily be trimmed (on both edges) in one hour.........	$30.00

SEE PERFORATED SLIP AND FRONT PAGES FOR DISCOUNT AND TERMS.

PAPER-HANGERS' TOOLS AND SUPPLIES.

RIDGELY'S NEW TRIMMER AND BRASS BOUND STRAIGHT EDGE.

This Trimmer will cut any thickness of paper, from a brown blank to the heaviest embossed and cartridge papers. It makes the cleanest and truest edge for butting. With it should be used Ridgely's brass-bound straight edge, which has a turned brass track on which the knife or trimmer runs. It is brass-bound on both edges, and can be used like any ordinary brass-bound straight edge, if desired. The whole outfit, which consists of trimmer, straight edge and strip of zinc for the top of table, is a great time and labor saver. With it there is no need of continually hunting

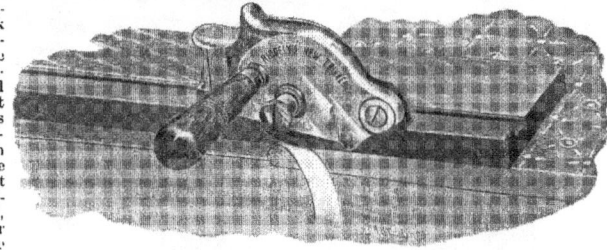

Showing Trimmer attached to Straight Edge.

knife or shears. When once the trimmer is attached to the straight edge, by sliding it on to the brass track from either end there is no necessity to remove it from the straight edge, from the commencement to the end of any job, and it is always ready for use. Great care should be taken in tacking the zinc to the table, so as to have it perfectly smooth. Each trimmer is nicely nickel-plated, wrapped in paper, and packed in neat paste board box.

No.						Each.
603	Outfit complete, with 6 foot straight edge and zinc					$7.70
607	"	"	7	"	"	"	8.10
608	"	"	8	"	"	"	8.50

RIDGELY'S BRASS-BOUND STRAIGHT EDGE ONLY.

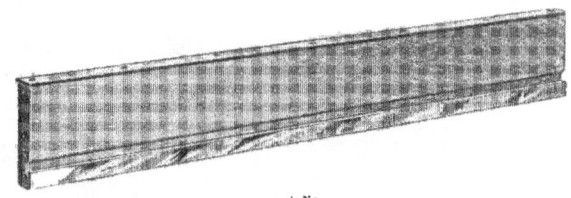

No.		Each.		No.		Each.
6	6 foot	$4.00		60	Trimmer only	$5.50
7	7 "	4.70		36	6 foot fine only	.40
8	8 "	5.40		37	7 " "	.50
				38	8 " "	.60

PLASTER FASTENER.

It is the needful thing for fastening loose plastering on walls or ceilings. The Fastener is a round piece of tin, countersunk for screw head, and concaved so that when the screw tightens the outer edge of the tin presses against the plaster. By putting a little plaster of Paris on screw head and around the tin, it leaves a smooth surface, and makes it as sound for paper or calcimine as a new wall.

No.	Per Gross.
670	$0.80

ADJUSTABLE TRESTLES.

No.	Per Set.
500	Weighing less than 5 lbs.; strong, made of hardwood. Can be folded for carrying, making a bundle 40 inches long and 2½ inches square	$3.80

SEE PERFORATED SLIP AND FRONT PAGES FOR DISCOUNT AND TERMS.

PAPER-HANGER'S PASTING TABLES.

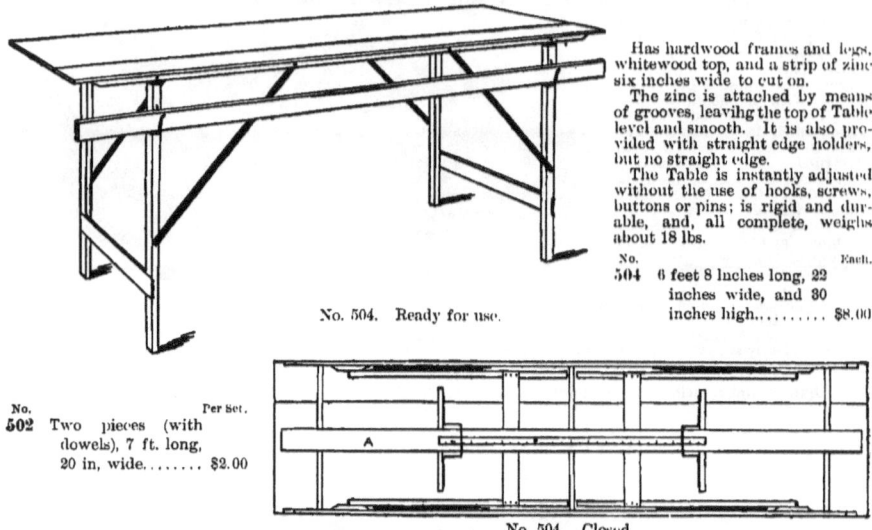

No. 504. Ready for use.

Has hardwood frames and legs, whitewood top, and a strip of zinc six inches wide to cut on.

The zinc is attached by means of grooves, leaving the top of Table level and smooth. It is also provided with straight edge holders, but no straight edge.

The Table is instantly adjusted without the use of hooks, screws, buttons or pins; is rigid and durable, and, all complete, weighs about 18 lbs.

No.		Each.
504	6 feet 8 inches long, 22 inches wide, and 30 inches high.........	$8.00

No.		Per Set.
502	Two pieces (with dowels), 7 ft. long, 20 in. wide.......	$2.00

No. 504. Closed.

ADJUSTABLE FOLDING TABLE.

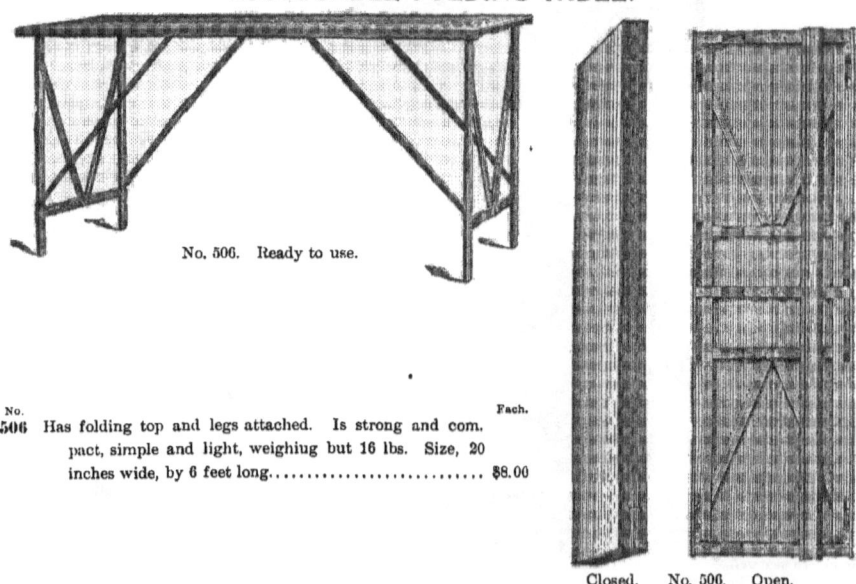

No. 506. Ready to use.

No.		Each.
506	Has folding top and legs attached. Is strong and compact, simple and light, weighing but 16 lbs. Size, 20 inches wide, by 6 feet long.........................	$8.00

Closed. No. 506. Open.

NOVELTY PASTING TABLE.

Patented April 3d, 1894.

OPEN READY FOR USE.

When open is 6 feet long and 22 inches wide, 30 inches in height, and stands firmly on the floor—has rubber tips on the legs to prevent slipping. Is the neatest and best thing ever invented for the purpose; saves all trouble and annoyance of barrels or boxes to put a pasting board on being carried to the rooms.

CLOSED.

When folded is a neat box lsss than 3 inches thick, which can be carried in any car, and no objection will be made to taking it into the best room in the house. Room for the tools inside. Also *made to fold lengthwise*, weight only about 15 pounds. Also made 7 feet in length.

No.	Each.
508...	$8.00

SEE PERFORATED SLIP AND FRONT PAGES FOR DISCOUNT AND TERMS.

PAPER-HANGERS' KNIVES.

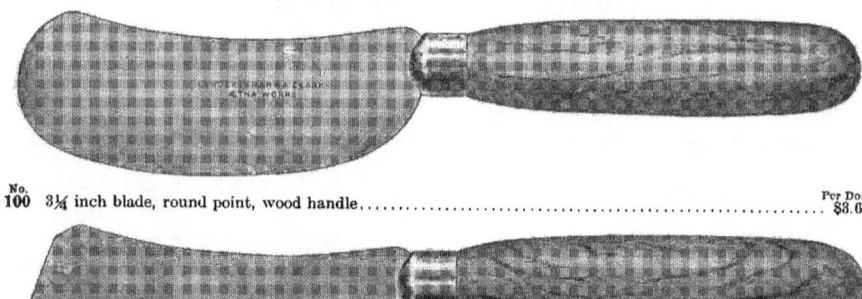

No.
100   3¼ inch blade, round point, wood handle...................................   Per Doz. $3.60

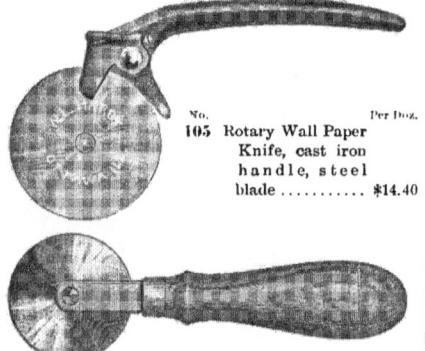

No.
115   3¼ inch blade, square point, wood handle ....   Per Doz. $3.60

No.
105   Rotary Wall Paper Knife, cast iron handle, steel blade ....   Per Doz. $14.40

No.
106   Rotary Casing Knife, hardwood handle, steel blade, hardwood protector to guide blade,   Per Doz. $19.20

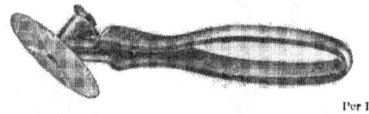

No.
107   Iron Handle Casing Knife ....   Per Doz. $10.80

No.
108   Trimming Knife, wood handle...........   Per Doz. $16.00

PERFECTION TRIMMING KNIFE.
Can be used either right or left hand, by easeing screw in handle.

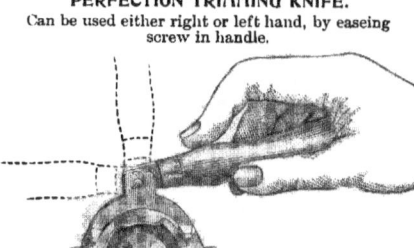

No.
109   Nickel plated............................   Per Doz. $24.00

WALL SCRAPERS.

No.
140   3½ inches wide, plain handle ....   Per Doz. $3.70

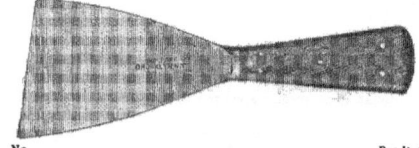

No.
135   3½ inches wide, polished handle..........   Per Doz. $10.50

SEE PERFORATED SLIP AND FRONT PAGES FOR DISCOUNT AND TERMS.

SEAM ROLLERS.

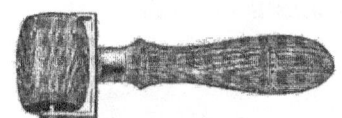

No.		Per Doz.
2	2 inch, flat rolling, brass frame, nickel plated,	$4.50
4	2 " barrel turned, " "	4.50
05	2 " " " spring axle, heavy cast iron frame, nickel plated	6.40

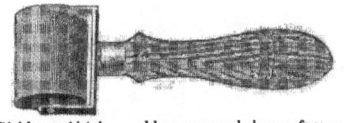

49	5½ in. x 1¼ in., rubber covered, brass frame, nickel plated	4.50
44	Same as 49, but heavy cast iron frame, nickel plated, spring axle	6.80

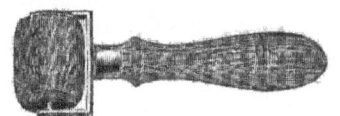

47	5½ in. x 1¼ in., rosewood, brass frame, nickel plated	4.50
46	Same as 47, heavy cast iron frame, nickel plated, spring axle	6.80

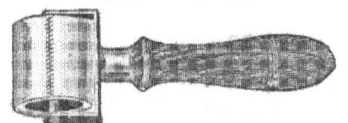

60	7½ in. x 2 in., covered with felt and muslin, patent handle	9.60
28	Same, heavier frame, padded and covered, spring axle, but no patent handle	16.00

39	5½ in. x 1¼ in., celluloid, brass frame, nickel plated	11.20
48	5½ in. x 1¼ in., ivory, heavy frame, nickel plated, spring axle	27.60

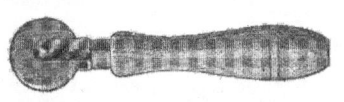

40	Square, ½ inch face, ivory seam roller, polished	16.00

SEAM ROLLERS.—Continued.

No.		Per Doz.
43	Rosewood, flat face	$10.80
45	Boxwood. "	10.00

41	Boxwood, bevel face	10.00

PAPER-HANGERS' BRUSHES.

PASTE BRUSHES.

Warranted Pure Bristles. Brass Bound.

No.		Per Doz.
116	Width 7 inch, gray center	$33.60
117	" 7 " all white	40.00
118	" 8 " " "	51.60

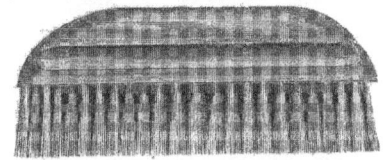

PAPER-HANGERS' SMOOTHING BRUSHES.

All Black. Wire Drawn.

No.		Per Doz.
131	10 inch, 2 Row	$10.40
132	12 " 2 "	13.60
129	10 " Soft black bristles, cemented	15.00

White Bristles. Cemented.

133	10 inch, 3 Row	20.80
134	12 " 3 "	26.40

Gray Russia Bristles. Wire Drawn.

135	10 inch, 4 Row	33.60
136	12 " 4 "	41.60

SEE PERFORATED SLIP AND FRONT PAGES FOR DISCOUNT AND TERMS.

SMOOTHING ROLLERS.

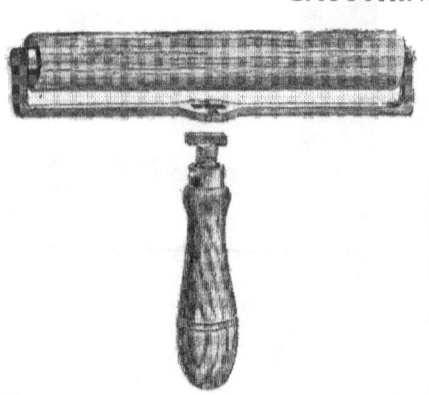

No.		Per Doz.
10	8 inch, polished wood, for ceiling, patent handle	$9.50
010	8 inch, polished wood, for ceiling, spring axle	10.00

No.		Per Doz.
35	4 inch, side arm, 1½ inch diameter........	$22.00
50	4½ inch, side arm, 1¾ inch diameter, spring axle...................	24.00

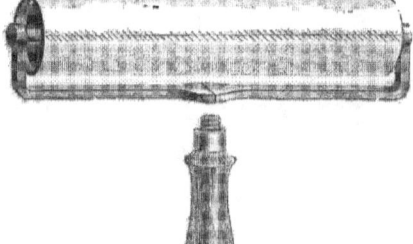

PLUMB BOB.

No.		Per Doz.
20	8 inch, covered with felt and muslin, patent handle	$27.00
26	Same as No. 20, nickel plated bearings, spring axle, plain handle................	30.00

No.		Per Doz.
1	Nickel Plated Screw Top, steel point..........	$8.00

LAKESIDE WALL PAPER HANGERS' PASTE.

Clean and strongly adhesive, always sweet and ready for use; no offensive odor.

Barrels of about 275 lbs ....per bbl. $4.00

SEE PERFORATED SLIP AND FRONT PAGES FOR DISCOUNT AND TERMS.

A NEW DEVICE

For Stippling, Stenciling, Frosting on Glass, and for paper-hangers' smoothing and seam rollers. Has had a practical test of five years' constant use, as the testimonials with directions on each roller will show. Made of Brass, in lengths two, five and eight inches, by one and three-quarter inches diameter.

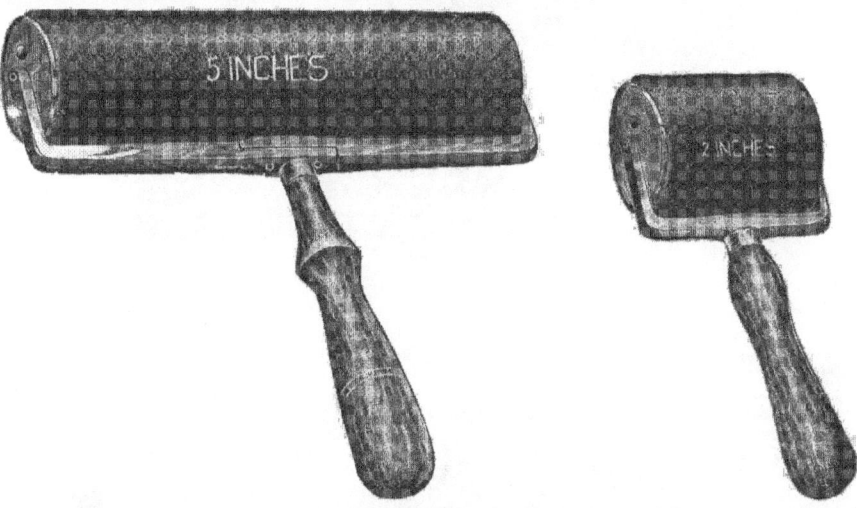

THE PRINCIPAL FEATURE OF THE ROLLER

Is, that it opens to receive the ends of the cloth or plush, and when closed draws the same tightly around the cylinder, clasping it firmly, and preventing any rotary or side slipping on the cylinder, leaving no seam—thereby overcoming all former objections, as well as trouble and waste of time in sewing, nailing or pasting cloth on rollers. The covering can be taken off, washed and replaced in a few moments, or will keep fresh for two days by placing the roller in its air tight box.

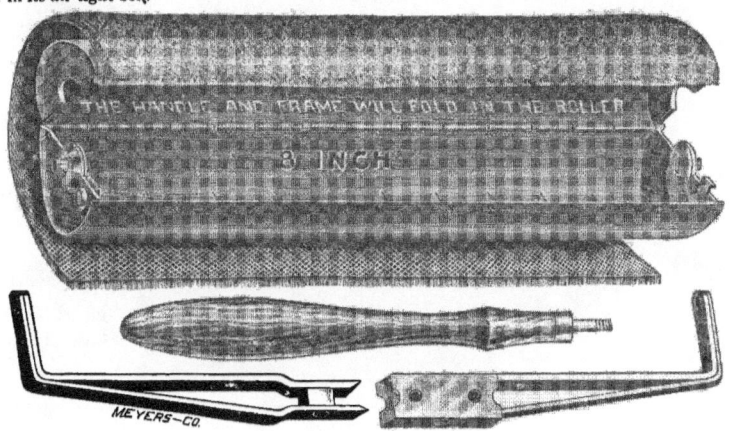

No.				
52	Two inch, in air tight box		Each,	$2.00
53	Five " " "		"	3.00
54	Eight " " "		"	4.00
55	Three rollers " "		Per set,	9.00

SEE PERFORATED SLIP AND FRONT PAGES FOR DISCOUNT AND TERMS.

STRAIGHT EDGES.

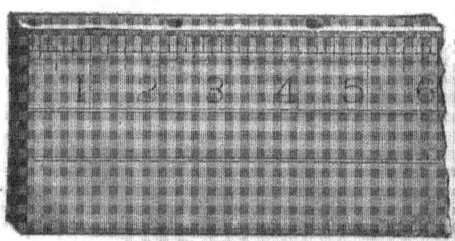

Nos. 506 and 507.

No.		Each.
506	6½ feet the best and cheapest made..	$1.90
507	7 " " " "	2.30

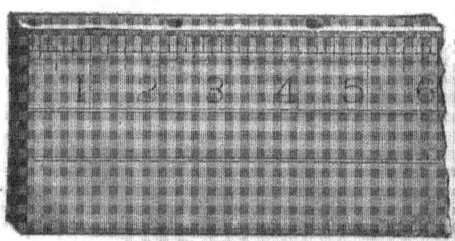

Nos. 106 and 208.

No.		
106	Pine, brass bound, graduated scale, 6 feet...	$8.00
208	Same, 8 feet long......	12.00

SHADE HANGERS' RULES.

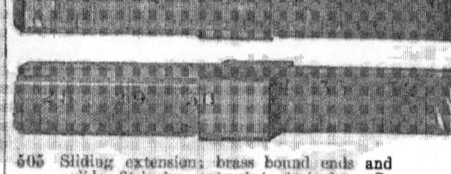

No.		Each.
505	Sliding extension; brass bound ends and slide; 31 inches. extends to 60 inches. So made that window can be measured without use of stepladder....	$1.60
606	37 inches, extends to 72 inches	8 18

PAPER HANGERS' SHEARS.

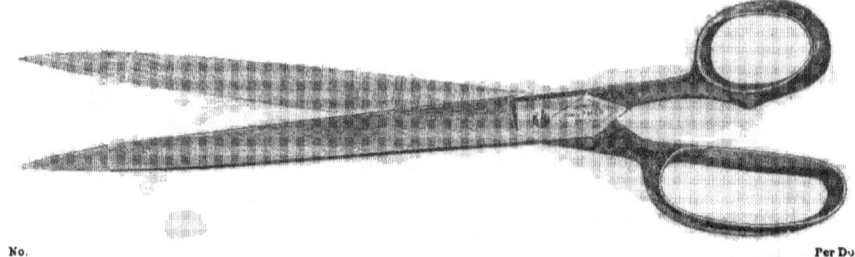

No.		Per Doz.
112	12 inch, heavy, nickel plated, japanned handles..	$20.00
114	14 " " " " "	27.00
116	16 " " " " "	38.00

SEE PERFORATED SLIP AND FRONT PAGES FOR DISCOUNT AND TERMS.

PUTTY KNIVES.

ALL SEVEN INCHES LONG.

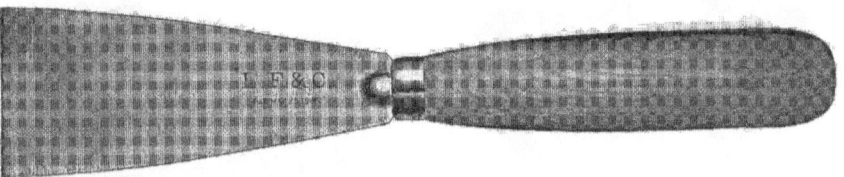

No. 800.

No.		Per Doz.
800	Plain beech handle, elastic steel blade, square point...	$2.70

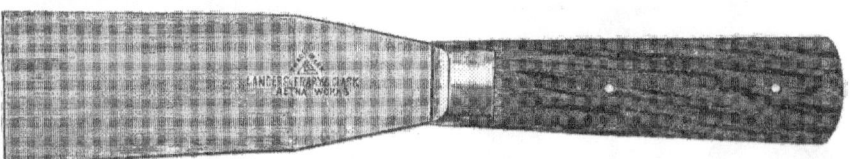

No. 980.

No.		Per Doz.
980	Coco handle, riveted, elastic steel blade, square point............................	$3.40

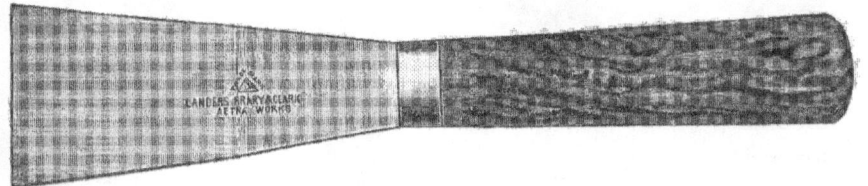

No. 9001.

No.		Per Doz.
9001	Solid handle, stiff steel blade, square point...	$3.60

GLASS CUTTERS.

No. 55.

No.		Per Doz.
55	Iron, steel point, diamondized wheel..	$1.00

No. 60.

No.		Per Doz.
60	Steel, wood handle, diamondized wheel..	$1.50

SEE PERFORATED SLIP AND FRONT PAGES FOR DISCOUNT AND TERMS.

PICTURE MOULDING HOOKS.

Packed in ¼ gross boxes except Nos. 123 and 127, which are packed one gross in a box.

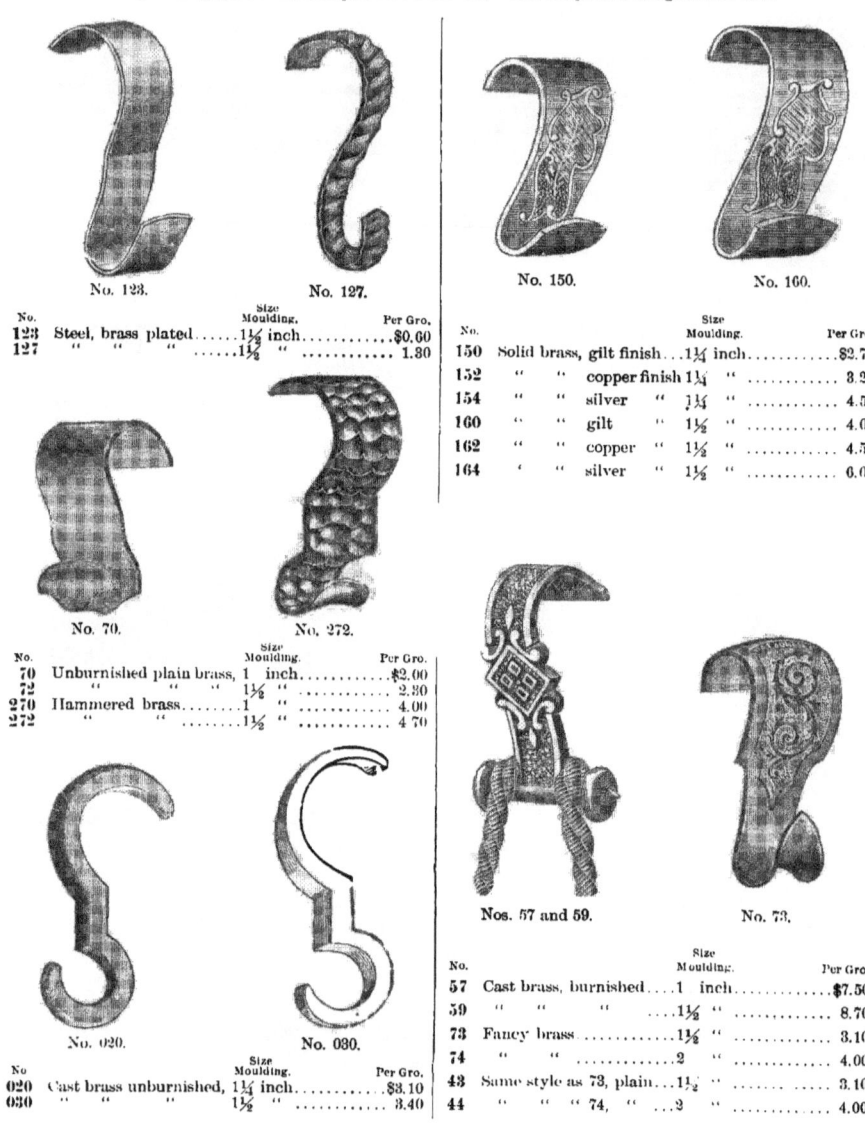

No. 123.   No. 127.   No. 150.   No. 160.

No.			Size Moulding.		Per Gro.
123	Steel, brass plated		1¼ inch		$0.60
127	" " "		1½ "		1.30

No.			Size Moulding.		Per Gro.
150	Solid brass, gilt finish		1¼ inch		$2.70
152	" "	copper finish	1¼ "		3.20
154	" "	silver	1¼ "		4.50
160	" "	gilt	1½ "		4.00
162	" "	copper	1½ "		4.50
164	" "	silver	1½ "		6.00

No. 70.   No. 272.

No.			Size Moulding.		Per Gro.
70	Unburnished plain brass,	1 inch			$2.00
72	" " "	1½ "			2.30
270	Hammered brass	1 "			4.00
272	" "	1½ "			4.70

Nos. 57 and 59.   No. 73.

No.			Size Moulding.		Per Gro.
57	Cast brass, burnished		1 inch		$7.50
59	" " "		1½ "		8.70
73	Fancy brass		1½ "		3.10
74	" "		2 "		4.00
43	Same style as 73, plain		1½ "		3.10
44	" " " 74, "		2 "		4.00

No. 020.   No. 030.

No			Size Moulding.		Per Gro.
020	Cast brass unburnished,		1¼ inch		$3.10
030	" " "		1½ "		3.40

SEE PERFORATED SLIP AND FRONT PAGES FOR DISCOUNT AND TERMS.

CROWN PICTURE HANGERS.

Most elegant in design and finish.

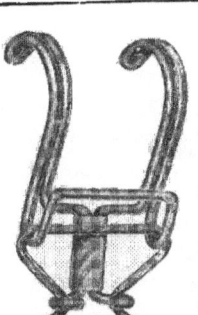

As shown by cuts, this is a device which locks the picture cord so that it cannot escape from nor slip upon the supports, keeping the picture in proper position and secure.

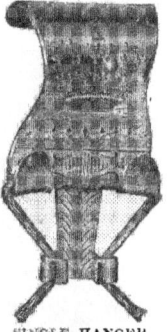

SINGLE HANGERS.

No.				Per Gross.
5	Figured brass,	for 1½ inch moulding		$5.00
3½	" "	" 2 " "		7.00
11	" and coppered, " 1½ "	"		6.00
9½	" " "	" 2 " "		8.50
17	" " nickeled	" 1½ " "		6.00
15½	" " "	" 2 " "		10.00
54	Plain Brass Wire,	" 1½ " "		4.00

No. 54.

SINGLE HANGER.

PORCELAIN PICTURE KNOBS.

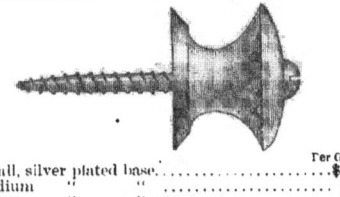

No.			Per Gross.
0	Small, silver plated base		$2.70
1	Medium " "		2.90
2	Large " "		3.00

WORSTED PICTURE CORD.
COLORS: GREEN, SCARLET, CRIMSON, BLUE.
In boxes of 30 yards.

No.	Per Doz. Boxes.
0	$2.56
1	2.88
2	3.84
3	5.20
4	6.48
5	
6	10.20

CROWN PICTURE NAIL.

No.		Per Gross.
016	Crown Nail	$2.70

WIRE PICTURE CORD.

Nos.

0 and 00

1 and 01

2 and 02

3 and 03

4 and 04

5 and 05

Full size cuts of wire. 25 yards in a coil.

SILVERED.		GILT.	
No.	Per Doz. Coils.	No.	Per Doz. Coils.
0	$0.46	00	$1.60
1	.70	01	2.70
2	1.16	02	3.90
3	1.40	03	5.80
4	1.90	04	6.80
5	2.30	05	9.00

BRASS PICTURE CHAIN.—No. 11. In yard lengths, one dozen in a box, with moulding hook and screw eye.................Per Doz. $1.08

SEE PERFORATED SLIP AND FRONT PAGES FOR DISCOUNT AND TERMS.

PICTURE NAILS.

All numbers packed ¼ gross in a box.

No.		Per Gross.
8	White porcelain center, plain rim	$2.10

Cut is full size of No. 8.

No.		Per Gross.
10	Solid porcelain head, ⅝ inch diameter	$4.30
11	Solid porcelain head, ¾ inch diameter	4.30

Cut is full size of No. 11.

No.		Per Gross.
9	White porcelain center, plain brass rim	$2.30
09	Ruby glass center, plain brass rim	3.00
19	Blue glass center, plain brass rim	3.00

Cut is full size of Nos. 9, 09 and 19.

No.		Per Gross.
5	Medallion center, fancy rim	$5.30
108	Medallion center, fancy rim	3.40

Cut is full size of No. 5.

No.		Per Gross.
90	Burnished brass center, enameled ground	$3.40
92	" " " " "	5.30

Small cut is full size of No. 90,
Large cut is full size of No. 92.

No.		Per Gross.
29	Ruby star, glass center, fancy burnished rim	$4.30
30	Green star, glass center, fancy burnished rim	4.30
31	Blue star, glass center, fancy burnished rim	4.30

Cut is full size of Nos. 29, 30 and 31.

No.		Per Gross.
100	Crystal glass center, plain rim	$3.40
101	Ruby rose glass center, plain rim	3.40
102	Green glass center, plain rim	3.40
103	Turquoise glass center, plain rim	3.40
104	Amber glass center, plain rim	3.40

Cut is full size of Nos. 100 to 104 inclusive.

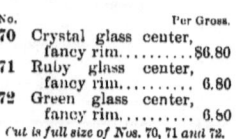

No.				Per Gross.
37	Crystal star glass center			$5.30
38	Ruby	"	"	5.30
39	Green	"	"	5.30
40	Blue	"	"	5.30
41	Turquoise star glass	"		5.30
42	Amber star glass center			5.30

Cut is full size of Nos. 37 to 42, inclusive.

No.		Per Gross.
70	Crystal glass center, fancy rim	$6.80
71	Ruby glass center, fancy rim	6.80
72	Green glass center, fancy rim	6.80

Cut is full size of Nos. 70, 71 and 72.

No.		Per Gross.
170	Crystal glass center, plain rim	$6.80

Cut is full size of No. 170.

Cut is full size of Nos. 47 and 48.

No.		Per Gross.
47	Crystal star center, fancy rim	$14.00
48	Ruby star center, fancy rim	14.00
55	Crystal star center, fancy rim, larger size	16.00

SCREW SUPPORTS.

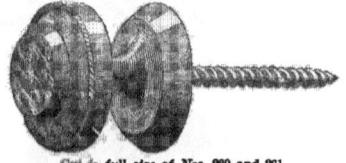

Cut is full size of Nos. 260 and 261.

No.		Per Gross.
260	Plain rim and base, silver glass center, with screw soldered on	$6.80
261	Plain rim and base, ruby glass center, with screw soldered on	6.80

SEE PERFORATED SLIP AND FRONT PAGES FOR DISCOUNT AND TERMS.

MALLEABLE IRON PICTURE NAILS.

Polished Brass Heads.

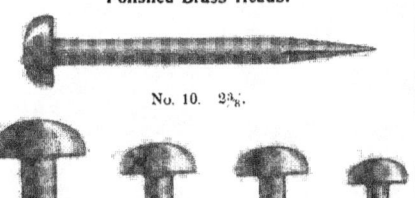

No. 10. 2⅜.

No. 10. 3⅜.   No. 10. 2⅜.   No. 10. 1⅞.   No. 10. 1⅝

No. 10	1⅝ inch......per gross	$1.60
" 10	1⅞ "	1.80
" 10	2⅜ "	2.20
" 10	3⅜ "	3.00

SCREW RINGS.

No. 18   ⅜ inch brass; one gross in a box...$0.38   Per Gross.

BRIGHT WIRE SCREW EYES.

Cuts exact size. Packed one gross in a box.
PRICES ARE PER GROSS.

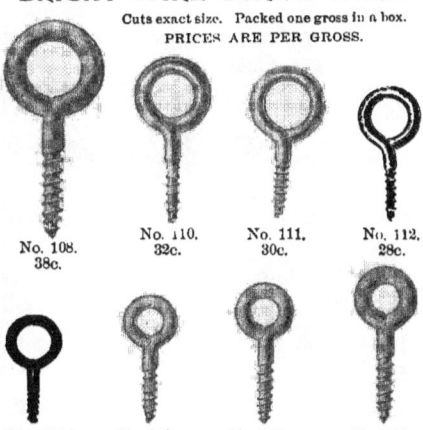

No. 108. 38c.   No. 110. 32c.   No. 111. 30c.   No. 112. 28c.

No. 214½. 20c.   No. 213. 24c.   No. 114. 24c.   No. 113. 26c.

PICTURE HANGING OUTFITS.

WITH PICTURE NAIL.

Full Size Cut

No cards to be broken, no parts out of place or lost. The Coil of Wire, Picture Nail and Screw Eyes are placed in Patent Folding Box, making a neat and very saleable article.

No.		
0914.	3 yds. No. 0 Wire, 1 Nail and 2 Screw Eyes.	
1913.	3 yds. " 1 Wire, 1 Nail and 2 Screw Eyes.	
2912.	3 yds. " 2 Wire, 1 Nail and 2 Screw Eyes.	
3911.	3 yds. " 3 Wire, 1 Nail and 2 Screw Eyes.	
4910.	3 yds. " 4 Wire, 1 Nail and 2 Screw Eyes.	
5908.	3 yds. " 5 Wire, 1 Nail and 2 Screw Eyes.	

PRICE LIST—PER DOZEN.

No.	0914	1913	2912	3911	4910	5908
	$0.60	.70	.80	1.00	1.20	1.50

Packed 3 dozen in a box. We do not break packages.

WITH PICTURE HOOKS.

Full Size Cut

Like the Picture Hanger with Nail this is a new article. The several parts are placed in our Patent Folding Box. The contents are printed on the outside, as represented in the cut.

No.		
0714.	3 yds. No. 0 Wire, 1 Hook and 2 Screw Eyes.	
1713.	3 yds. " 1 Wire, 1 Hook and 2 Screw Eyes.	
2712.	3 yds. " 2 Wire, 1 Hook and 2 Screw Eyes.	
3711.	3 yds. " 3 Wire, 1 Hook and 2 Screw Eyes.	
4710.	3 yds. " 4 Wire, 1 Hook and 2 Screw Eyes.	
5708.	3 yds. " 5 Wire, 1 Hook and 2 Screw Eyes.	

PRICE LIST—PER DOZEN.

No.	0714	1713	2712	3711	4710	5708
	$0.60	.70	.80	1.00	1.20	1.50

Packed 3 dozen in a box. We do not break packages.

SEE PERFORATED SLIP AND FRONT PAGES FOR DISCOUNT AND TERMS.

UPHOLSTERY HARDWARE.

WOOD CORNICE POLES.

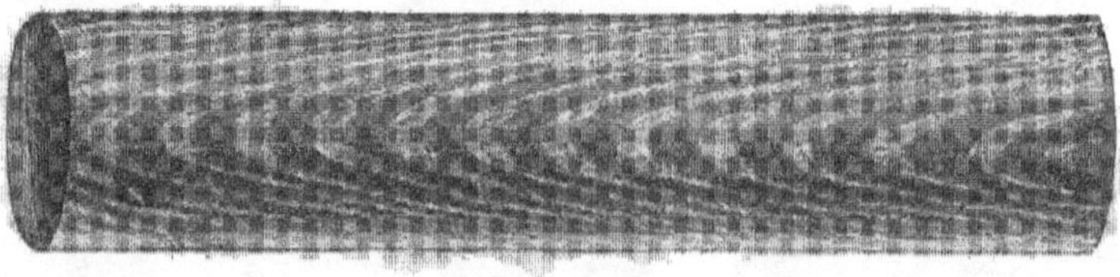

WELL FINISHED IN IMITATION OF ANTIQUE OAK, EBONY, MAHOGANY, WALNUT AND ASH, 4, 5, 8 AND 12 FEET LONG.

No.	Description.	Length.	Per Doz.	No.	Description.	Length.	Per Doz.
141	1 inch Antique Oak	4 feet,	$1.08	41	1⅜ inch Antique Oak	4 feet,	$1.08
142	″ Ebony	″	1.08	42	″ Ebony	″	1.08
143	″ Mahogany	″	1.08	43	″ Mahogany	″	1.08
144	″ Walnut	″	1.08	44	″ Walnut	″	1.08
145	″ Ash	″	1.08	45	″ Ash	″	1.08
151	″ Antique Oak	5 feet,	1.20	51	″ Antique Oak	5 feet,	1.20
152	″ Ebony	″	1.20	52	″ Ebony	″	1.20
153	″ Mahogany	″	1.20	53	″ Mahogany	″	1.20
154	″ Walnut	″	1.20	54	″ Walnut	″	1.20
155	″ Ash	″	1.20	55	″ Ash	″	1.20
181	″ Antique Oak	8 feet,	3.36	81	″ Antique Oak	8 feet,	3.36
182	″ Ebony	″	3.36	82	″ Ebony	″	3.36
183	″ Mahogany	″	3.36	83	″ Mahogany	″	3.36
184	″ Walnut	″	3.36	84	″ Walnut	″	3.36
185	″ Ash	″	3.36	85	″ Ash	″	3.36
1121	″ Antique Oak	12 feet,	5.04	121	″ Antique Oak	12 feet,	5.04
1122	″ Ebony	″	5.04	122	″ Ebony	″	5.04
1123	″ Mahogany	″	5.04	123	″ Mahogany	″	5.04
1124	″ Walnut	″	5.04	124	″ Walnut	″	5.04
1125	″ Ash	″	5.04	125	″ Ash	″	5.04

CORRUGATED WHITE ENAMELED POLES.

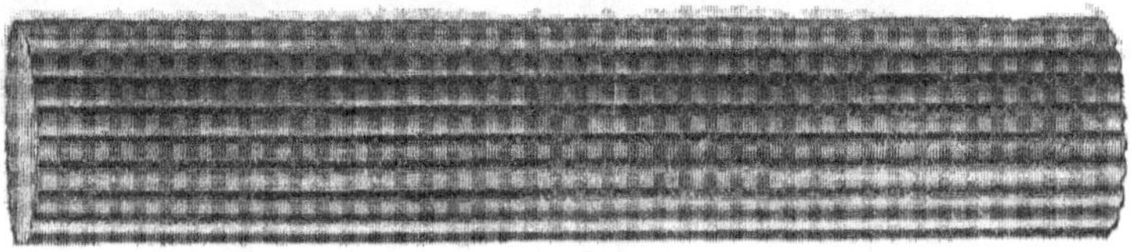

No.	Description	Per Doz.
158	1 inch in diameter by 5 feet long	$2.40
1108	1 ″ ″ 10 ″	4.80
1128	1 ″ ″ 12 ″	5.76
58	1⅜ ″ ″ 5 ″	3.00
108	1⅜ ″ ″ 10 ″	6.00
128	1⅜ ″ 12 ″	8.64

BRASS COVERED POLES.

No.	Description	Per Doz.
157	1 inch in diameter by 5 feet long, plain brass	$3.60
187	1 ″ ″ 8 ″ ″	5.76
1127	1 ″ ″ 12 ″ ″	8.64
57	1⅜ ″ ″ 5 ″ ″	5.20
87	1⅜ ″ ″ 8 ″ ″	8.64
127	1⅜ ″ ″ 12 ″ ″	12.96
126	1⅜ ″ ″ 12 ″ spiral brass	28.80

SEE PERFORATED SLIP AND FRONT PAGES FOR DISCOUNT AND TERMS.

WOOD TRIMMED CORNICE POLES COMPLETE.

Each set consists of one 5 foot by 1⅜ inch pole, one pair of ends, one pair of brackets and ten rings.
Packed two dozen sets in a case. We do not break cases.

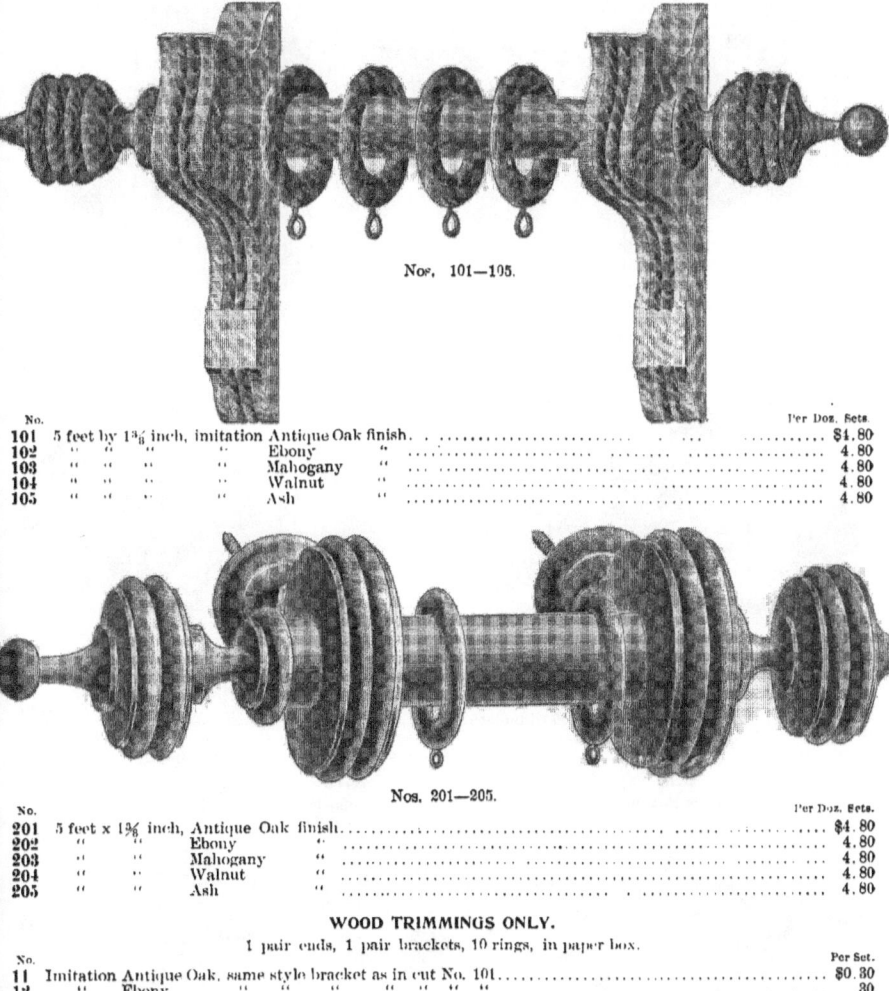

Nos. 101—105.

No.						Per Doz. Sets.
101	5 feet by 1⅜ inch, imitation	Antique Oak finish				$4.80
102	" " "	"	Ebony	"		4.80
103	" " "	"	Mahogany	"		4.80
104	" " "	"	Walnut	"		4.80
105	" " "	"	Ash	"		4.80

Nos. 201—205.

No.					Per Doz. Sets.
201	5 feet x 1⅜ inch, Antique Oak finish				$4.80
202	" "	Ebony	"		4.80
203	" "	Mahogany	"		4.80
204	" "	Walnut	"		4.80
205	" "	Ash	"		4.80

WOOD TRIMMINGS ONLY.

1 pair ends, 1 pair brackets, 10 rings, in paper box.

No.			Per Set.
11	Imitation Antique Oak, same style bracket as in cut No. 101		$0.30
12	" Ebony, " " " " " " "		.30
13	" Mahogany, " " " " " " "		.30
14	" Walnut, " " " " " " "		.30
15	" Ash " " " " " " "		.30
21	" Antinque Oak Finish, same style bracket as in cut No. 201		.30
22	" Ebony " " " " " " "		.30
23	" Mahogany " " " " " " "		.30
24	" Walnut " " " " " " "		.30
25	" Ash " " " " " " "		.30

SEE PERFORATED SLIP AND FRONT PAGES FOR DISCOUNT AND TERMS.

WOOD CORNICE POLES WITH BRASS TRIMMINGS COMPLETE.

POLES ARE 1⅜ INCHES IN DIAMETER, 4 FEET LONG, TRIMMINGS WITH 8 RINGS.

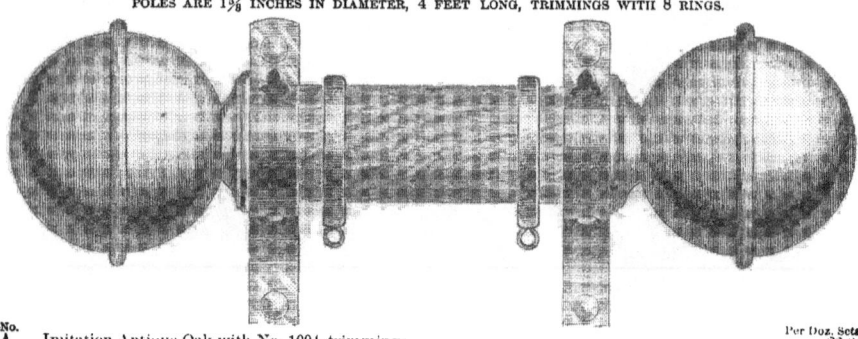

No.					Per Doz. Sets.
A	Imitation Antique Oak with No. 1004 trimmings				$2.84
B	"	Ebony	"	"	2.84
C	"	Mahogany	"	"	2.84
D	"	Walnut	"	"	2.84
E	"	Ash	"	"	2.84

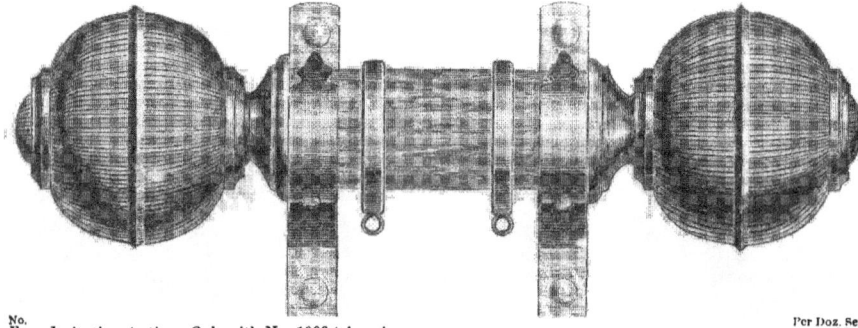

No.					Per Doz. Sets.
F	Imitation Antique Oak with No. 1006 trimmings				$2.84
G	"	Ebony	"	"	2.84
H	"	Mahogany	"	"	2.84
I	"	Walnut	"	"	2.84
J	"	Ash	"	"	2.84

Corrugated White Enameled Poles with Silver Trimmings Complete. Poles are 1⅜ inches by 4 feet. Trimmings, silver ends with brass rings and brackets.

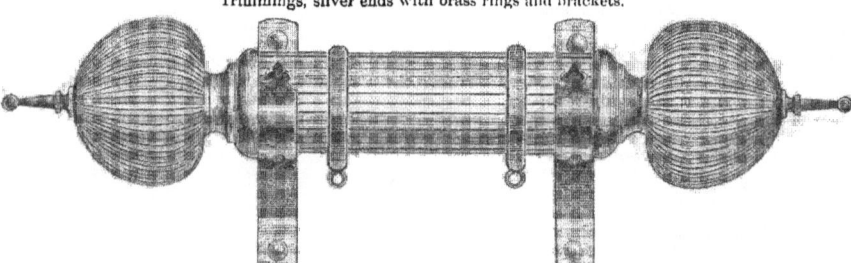

No.		Per Doz. Sets.
601	White Enamel Pole, Silver ball, with Brass tip and collar	$8.00

SEE PERFORATED SLIP AND FRONT PAGES FOR DISCOUNT AND TERMS.

BRASS CORNICE POLE TRIMMINGS.
FOR 1 INCH POLES.

Packed one set in box.   Set comprises one pair ends, one pair brackets, 10 rings.

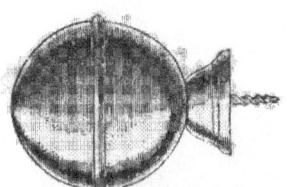

No. 1000.   **1 inch, full size**

No. 1100.   1 inch, full size.

No.		Per Set.
1000	For 1 inch pole, polished brass, spring bracket, polished rings.............................,.........**$0.20**
1100	" " " " " " " " ...., **.37**

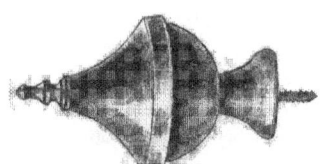

No. 1102.   1 inch, ½ size.

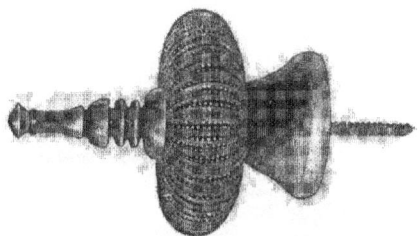

No. 1103.   1. inch, full size.

No.		Per Set.
1102	For 1 inch pole, polished brass, spring bracket, polished ring, swing eye **$0.37**
1103	" " " silver cast brass tip, rosette bracket, polished ring........................ .... **.40**

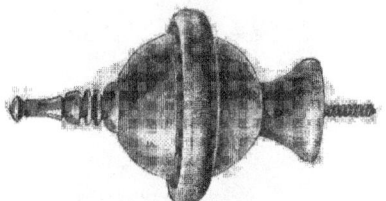

No. 1104.   1 inch, half size.

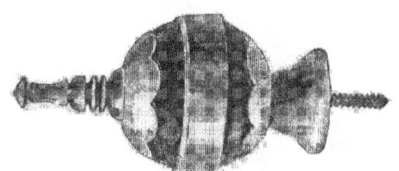

No. 1105.   1 inch, half size,

No.		Per Set.
1104	For 1 inch pole, very heavy polished brass ends, brackets and rings........................ ... .**$0.60**
1105	" " " polished brass centre, frosted silver ends, cast brass tip, extra polished bracket and rings .... **.70**

SEE PERFORATED SLIP AND FRONT PAGES FOR DISCOUNT AND TERMS.

BRASS CORNICE POLE TRIMMINGS.—Continued.

FOR 1½ INCH POLES.

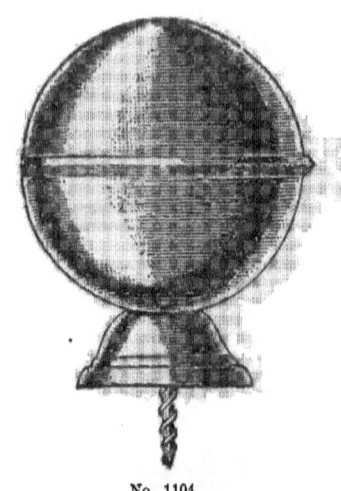

No. 1104.   No. 1006.

No.		Per Set.
1004	For 1½ inch pole; polished brass ends, brass plated spring brackets, light oval brass tube rings, bracket and ring gilt finish...$0.15	
1006	For 1½ inch pole; brass ends, brass plated spring brackets, light oval brass tube rings, all gilt finish... .15	

No. 1008.   No. 1210.

No.		Per Set.
1008	For 1½ inch pole; polished brass ends, brass plated spring brackets, oval brass tube rings, all polished.$0.25	
1210	For 1½ inch pole; brass ends, polished band, brass plated spring brackets, polished, light oval brass tube rings, gilt finish... .25	

SEE PERFORATED SLIP AND FRONT PAGES FOR DISCOUNT AND TERMS.

BRASS CORNICE POLE TRIMMINGS.—Continued.

FOR 1½ INCH POLES.

No. 1212. Cut full size.   No. 1214.

No.		Per Set.
1212	For 1½ inch pole, polished brass bottom, fancy brass top, brass plated spring bracket, light tube ring, gilt finish	$0.30
1214	For 1½ inch pole, plain polished brass end, spring bracket, polished ring	.32

No. 1216. Cut ⅔ size.   No. 1218. Cut ⅔ size.

No.		Per Set.
1216	For 1½ inch pole, all brass spring bracket, polished ring	$0.40
1218	" " " brass polished ends and bracket, polished ring	.44

SEE PERFORATED SLIP AND FRONT PAGES FOR DISCOUNT AND TERMS.

BRASS CORNICE POLE TRIMMINGS—Continued.
FOR 1½ INCH POLES.

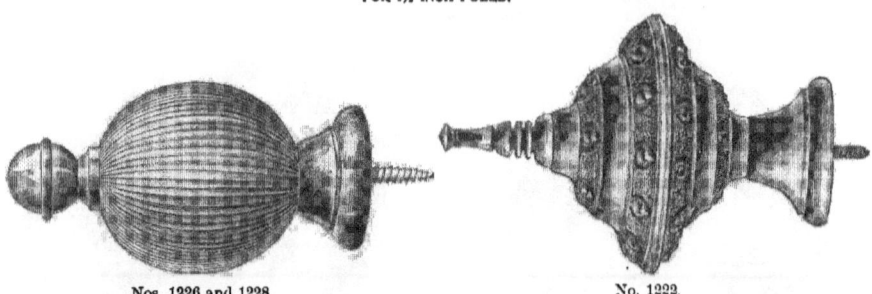

Nos. 1226 and 1228.   No. 1222.

No.				Per Set.
1222	For 1½ inch pole, brass end, polished tip and collar, polished ring and bracket...................	$0.50
1226	" " " corrugated silver end, polished tip and collar, polished ring and bracket...........	.50
1228	" " " copper " " " " " " " "	.50

No. 1230.

No. 1244.

No.				Per Set.
1230	For 1½ inch pole, gold top, silver bottom, polished brass bracket and ring.........................	$0.70
1244	" " " " " " " silver rosette on tip, solid brass bracket, heavy brass ring..	.84

SEE PERFORATED SLIP AND FRONT PAGES FOR DISCOUNT AND TERMS.

BRASS CORNICE POLE TRIMMINGS.—Continued.
FOR 1½ INCH POLES.

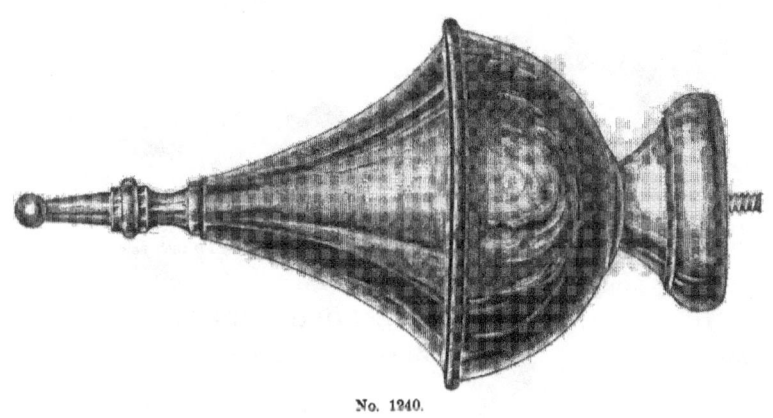

No. 1240.

No.		Per Set.
1240	For 1¼ inch pole, all gold, solid brass bracket, heavy brass ring..............................	$0.84

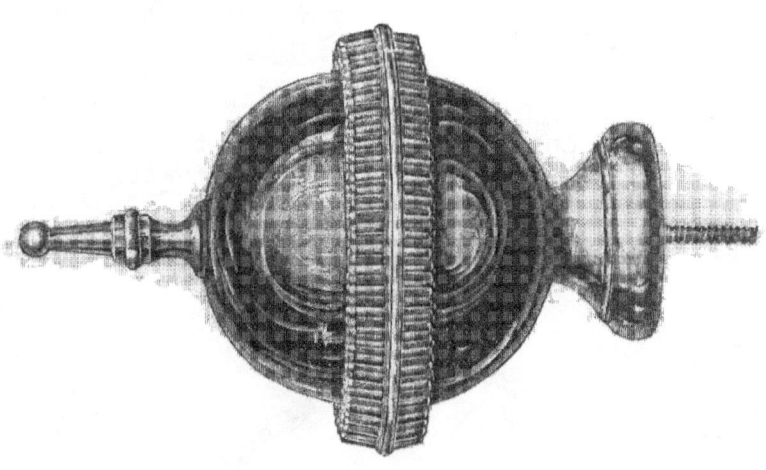

No. 1242.

No.		Per Set.
1242	For 1¼ inch pole, all gold, with silver band, solid brass bracket, heavy brass ring..............	$0.84

SEE PERFORATED SLIP AND FRONT PAGES FOR DISCOUNT AND TERMS.

ADJUSTABLE ANGLE JOINTS.

For 1 inch and 1⅜ inch poles.

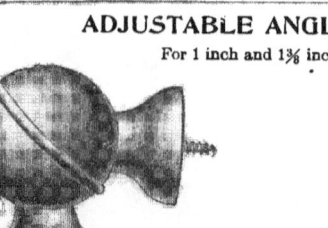

No.		Per Doz.
010	For 1 inch pole, adjustable for bay windows, corners, etc., brass, polished..............$1.44	

No.		Per Doz.
10	Same as 010, for 1⅜ inch pole..............	$1.60

CORNICE POLE SOCKETS.

For 1 inch and 1⅜ inch poles.

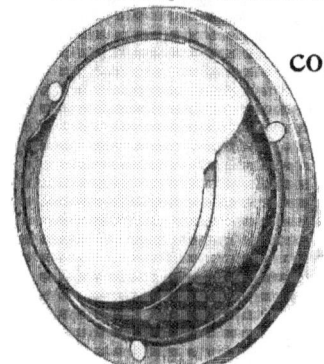

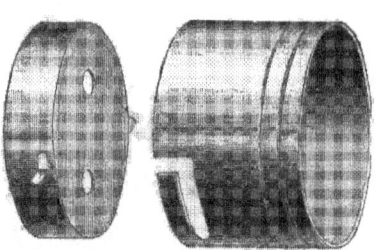

No.		Per Doz. Pairs.
010	For 1 inch pole; one end open, brass, polished.	$0.48
10	For 1⅜ inch pole, otherwise same as 010.....	.48

No.		Per Doz. Pairs.
026	For 1 inch pole; bayonet lock, brass, polished.	$1.36
26	For 1⅜ " " " " "	1.36

CORNICE POLE RINGS.

For 1 inch and 1⅜ inch poles.

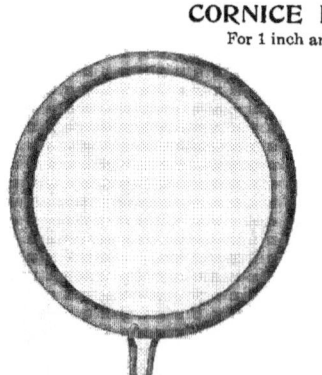

No.		Per 100.
061	1¼ inch diameter ; light oval, brass tube ring, gilt finish........................$1.20	
61	1¾ inch diameter, otherwise same as 061....	1.20

No.		Per Doz.
45	Day's patent traverse, heavy brass tube, polished ; for 1⅜ inch pole	$1.80

SEE PERFORATED SLIP AND FRONT PAGES FOR DISCOUNT AND TERMS.

PROJECTION AND EXTENSION POLE BRACKETS.

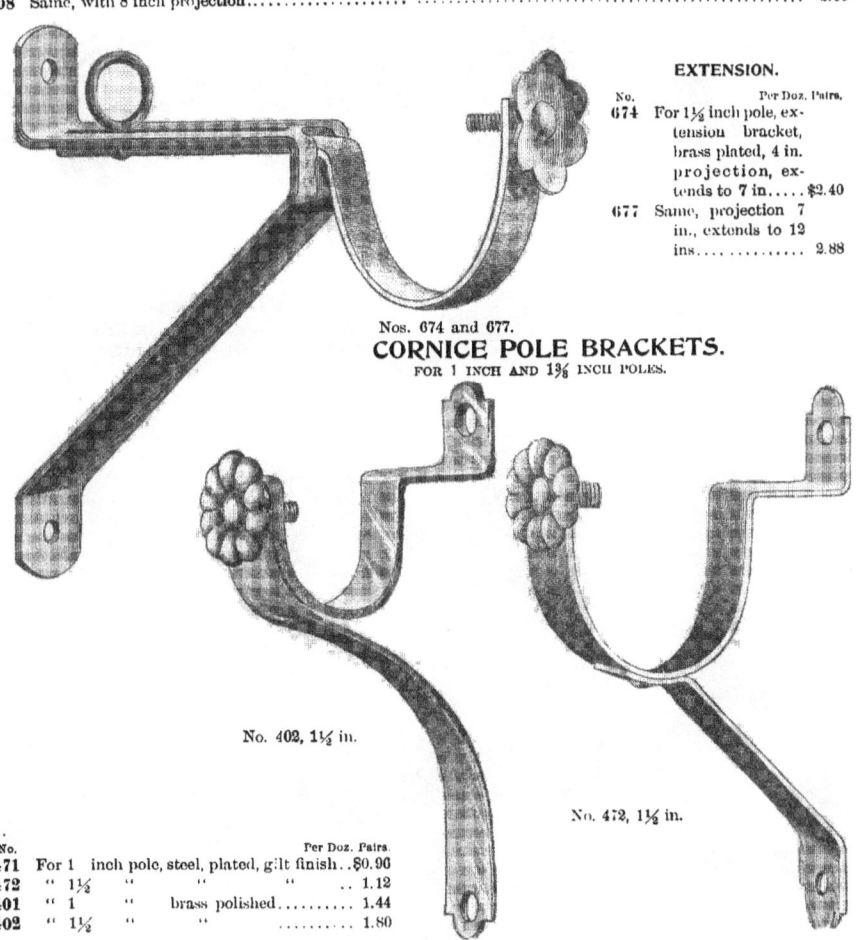

PROJECTION.—Nos. 506 and 508.

No.		Per Doz. Pairs.
506	For 1½ inch pole, brass plated, polished, 6 inch projection	$1.76
508	Same, with 8 inch projection	2.00

EXTENSION.

No.		Per Doz. Pairs.
674	For 1½ inch pole, extension bracket, brass plated, 4 in. projection, extends to 7 in	$2.40
677	Same, projection 7 in., extends to 12 ins	2.88

Nos. 674 and 677.

CORNICE POLE BRACKETS.
FOR 1 INCH AND 1⅜ INCH POLES.

No. 402, 1½ in.

No. 472, 1½ in.

No.		Per Doz. Pairs.
471	For 1 inch pole, steel, plated, gilt finish	$0.96
472	" 1½ " " "	1.12
401	" 1 " brass polished	1.44
402	" 1½ " "	1.80

Brass Drapery and Curtain Chains.

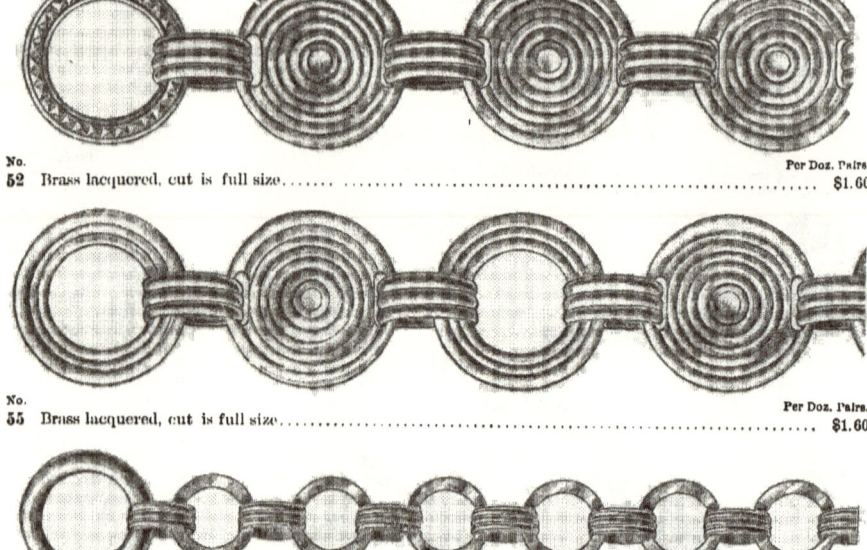

No.
52 Brass lacquered, cut is full size... Per Doz. Pairs. $1.60

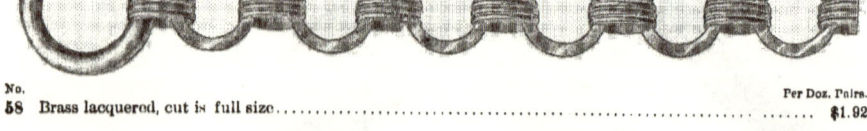

No.
55 Brass lacquered, cut is full size... Per Doz. Pairs. $1.60

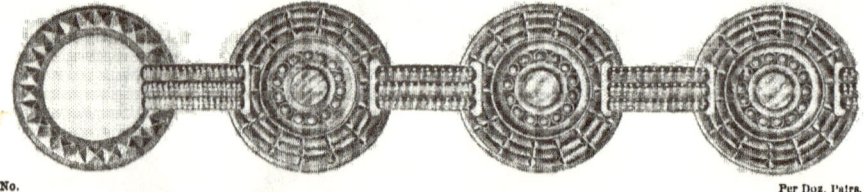

No.
58 Brass lacquered, cut is full size... Per Doz. Pairs. $1.92

No.
61 Brass lacquered, cut is full size... Per Doz. Pairs. $2.24

No.
43 Brass lacquered, cut is full size... Per Doz. Pairs. $2.24

SEE PERFORATED SLIP AND FRONT PAGES FOR DISCOUNT AND TERMS.

DRAPERY AND CURTAIN CHAINS.—Continued.

WOVEN WIRE GOODS. ALL BRASS WIRE.

CUTS SHOW EXACT SIZE OF COIL.

THE BEAUTIFUL EFFECT OF THESE GOODS IS DUE ENTIRELY TO THE COLORINGS.—THE CUTS FAIL TO DO THEM JUSTICE. THEY HAVE A FINE, SILKY APPEARANCE.

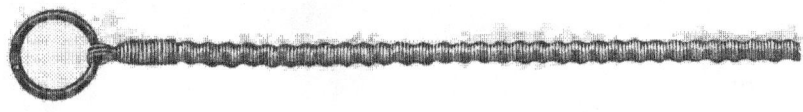

No.		Per Doz. Pairs.
115	Gilt finish	$1.80
116	Silver finish	1.80
117	Old Gold finish	1.80
118	Olive finish	1.80
119	Blue finish	1.80

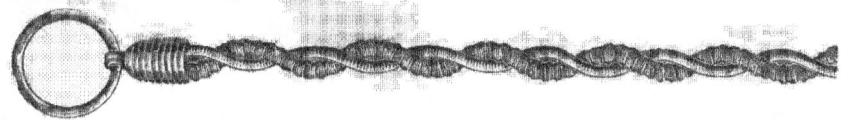

No.		Per Doz. Pairs.
120	Brass finish	$2.88
121	Silver finish	2.88
122	Silver and Blue finish	2.88
123	Silver and Olive finish	2.88
124	Brass and Silver finish	2.88

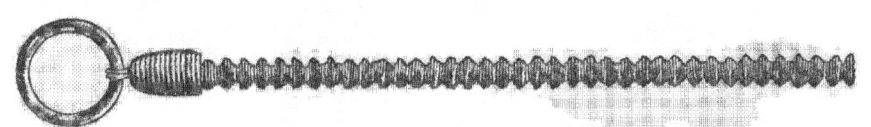

No.		Per Doz. Pairs.
125	Brass finish	$2.88
126	Silver "	2.88
127	Gold "	2.88
128	Blue "	2.88

No.		Per Doz. Pairs.
129	Silver and Brass finish	$4.70
130	" " Blue "	4.70
131	" " Olive "	4.70
132	" " Gold "	4.70

SEE PERFORATED SLIP AND FRONT PAGES FOR DISCOUNT AND TERMS.

VESTIBULE HARDWARE.

BRASS ROD.

No.							Per 100 Feet.
4	Brass covered rod; ¼ inch, 12 foot lengths..						$3.40
14	"	plated	"	¼	"	"	2.00
8	"	covered	"	⅜	"	"	6.00
88	"	plated	"	⅜	"	"	4.00

Special price on 500 feet of a number.

CORNICE POLE AND ROD RING.

No.		Per Gross.
07	Rod ring; brass plated, gilt finish; for ⅜ inch rod	$1 00
08	Rod ring; brass plated, gilt finish; for ¼ inch rod	1.00

INSIDE SOCKET.

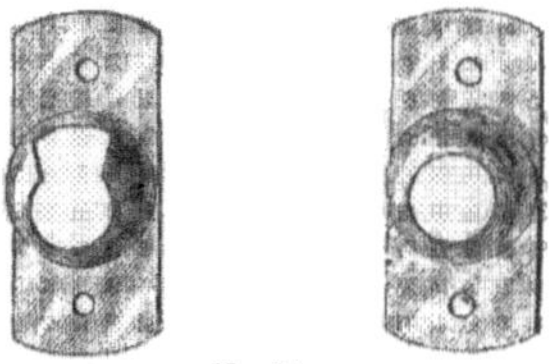

No. 01

No.		Per Doz. Pairs.
01	Socket for ¼ inch rod; brass polished	$0.24
11	" ⅜ " "	24

INSIDE BRACKETS.

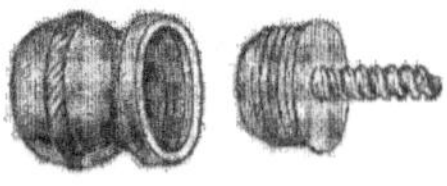

No.		Per Doz. Pairs.
02	Brackets for ¼ inch rod; brass polished	$0.80
12	" ⅜ " "	90

OUTSIDE BRACKETS.

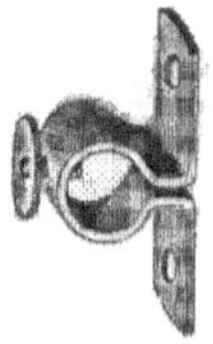

No.		Per Doz. Pairs.
03	Brackets for ¼ inch rod; brass polished	$0.54
13	" ⅜ " "	54

OUTSIDE BRACKETS.—Continued.

No.		Per Doz. Pairs.
04	Bracket and ends for ¼ inch rod; polished brass	$0.60
14	Same for ⅜ inch rod	80

PROJECTION BRACKETS.

No.		Per Doz. Pairs.
05	Projection bracket for ¼ inch rod; 2 inch projection, brass polished	$1.40
15	Projection bracket for ⅜ inch rod; 2 inch projection, brass polished	1.50

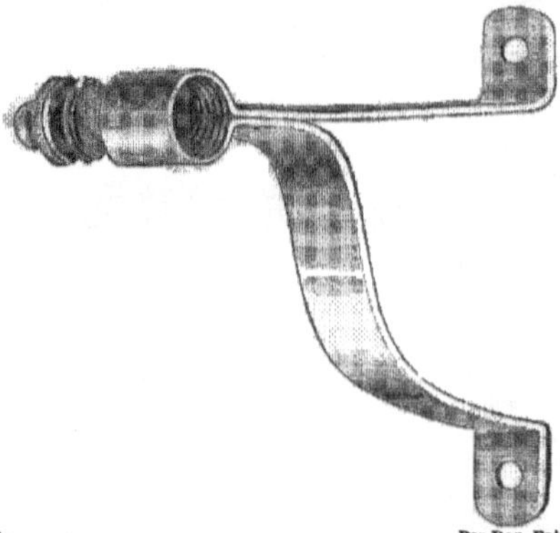

No.		Per Doz. Pairs.
25	Projection bracket for ⅜ inch rod; 2½ inch projection, brass polished	$2.00

PREMIER BRASS ROD BRACKETS.

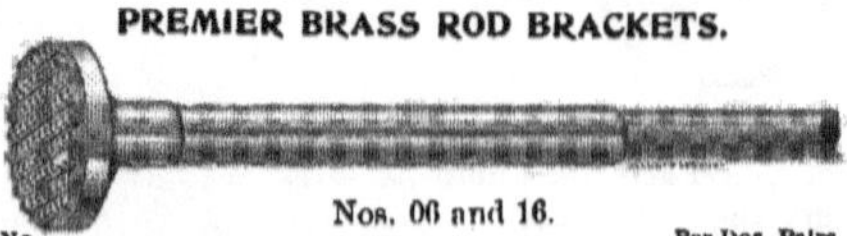

Nos. 06 and 16.

No.		Per Doz. Pairs.
06	Polished brass, 3 inches long, with rubber face, for ¼ inch rod	$2.00
16	Same for ⅜ inch rod	2.40

SEE PERFORATED SLIP AND FRONT PAGES FOR DISCOUNT AND TERMS.

VESTIBULE ROD CUTTER.

For cutting brass rod. Will cut $\frac{1}{8}$ to $\frac{3}{8}$ inch wire.

This rod cutter is the best, and by far the cheapest on the market. The above cut represents the complete machine, and we give below cuts representing all the different parts.

The cutting dies are made from the best cast steel, carefully tempered, and of such proportions as to secure the greatest strength and durability.

An important feature, which will commend itself to the customer, is the interchangeability of the parts, enabling the owner to replace a damaged or broken part readily, and at slight cost.

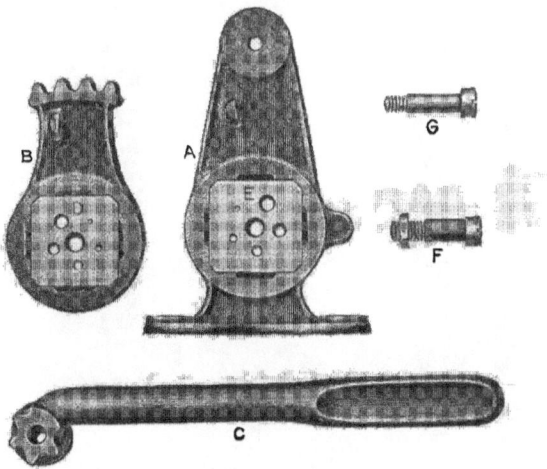

No.		Each.
20	Complete for $\frac{1}{4}$ inch and $\frac{3}{8}$ inch rod...	$7.00

When ordering parts separately, order by letter, as given in above cuts.

SEE PERFORATED SLIP AND FRONT PAGES FOR DISCOUNT AND TERMS.

TELESCOPE EXTENSION VESTIBULE RODS.

SPRING EXTENSION VESTIBULE RODS.

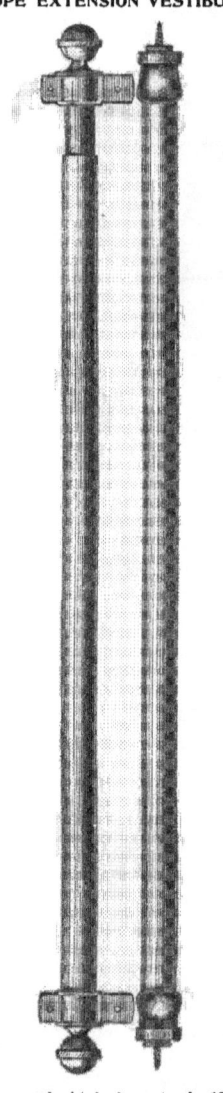

Nos. 137, 138 and 139 with outside brackets.

Nos. 137, 138 and 139 with inside brackets.

No.					Per Doz.
144	Telescope rod, ¼ inch, extends 12 to 24 inches; inside and outside brackets with each rod				$2.00
244	Telescope rod, ¼ inch, extends 24 to 44 inches; inside and outside brackets with each rod				2.50

No.					Per Doz.
137	Spring rod, ¼ inch, extends 15 to 22 inches,				$2.40
138	"	¼ "	"	22 to 30 "	2.80
139	"	¼ "	"	30 to 40 "	3.50

SEE PERFORATED SLIP AND FRONT PAGES FOR DISCOUNT AND TERMS.

TASSEL HOOKS.

Packed ¼ gross in a box.—Cut shows full size.

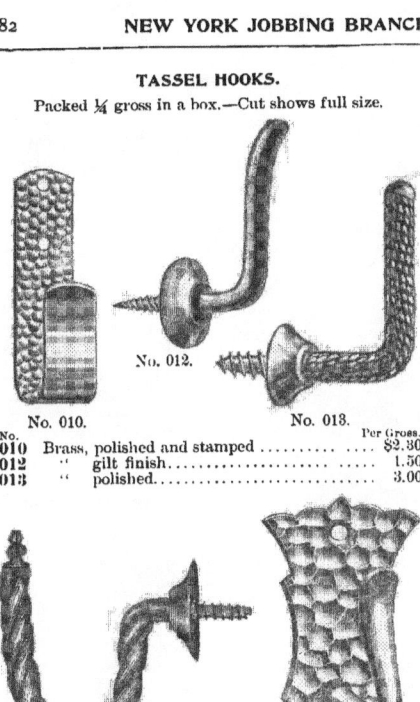

No. 012.

No. 010.   No. 013.

No.		Per Gross.
010	Brass, polished and stamped	$2.30
012	" gilt finish	1.50
013	" polished	3.00

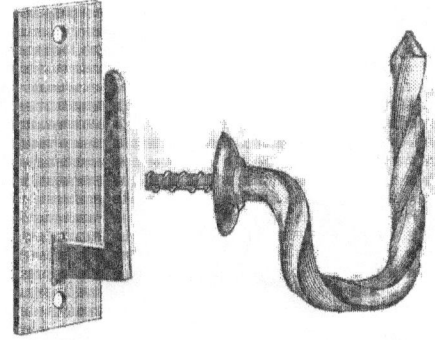

No. 011.   No. 015.

No.		Per Gross.
011	Twisted brass, polished	$3.80
015	Hammered " "	4.30

No. 016.   No. 020.

No.		Per Gross.
016	Brass, polished, wrought hook	$6.00
020	Extra heavy twisted brass, polished	6.50

DRAPERY HOOKS.

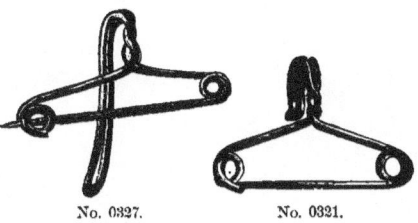

No. 0327.   No. 0321.

No.		Per Gross.
0321	Heavy brassed wire; point of hook being bent inward gives secure hold on eye of ring,	$0.30
0327	Heavy brassed wire	32

No.		
305	Made of light spring brass wire, ⅜ inch ring	$0.80

ESCUTCHEON PINS.

Packed 1,000 in a box.

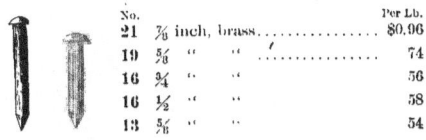

No.				Per Lb.
21	⅞ inch, brass			$0.96
19	⅝	"	"	74
16	¾	"	"	56
16	½	"	"	58
13	⅝	"	"	54

BRASS SCREWS.

Packed one gross in a box.

No.		Per Gross.
06	⅝ inch, brass, extra quality	$0.48

UPHOLSTERY NAILS.

Packed 1,000 in a box.

No. 137.   No. 137½.   No. 42.   No. 43.   No. 41.

No.		Per 1,000.
137	China nail	$1.10
137½	Tin disc for 137 nail	50
43	Brass nail	64
42	"	74
41	"	1.10

SEE PERFORATED SLIP AND FRONT PAGES FOR DISCOUNT AND TERMS.

BRASS SHOULDER HOOKS.

One gross in a box.

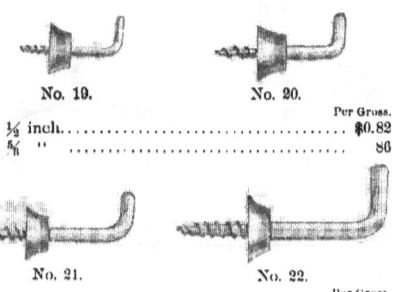

No. 19. No. 20.

No.			Per Gross.
19	½ inch		$0.82
20	⅝ "		86

No. 21. No. 22.

No.			Per Gross.
21	¾ inch		$1.02
22	1 "		1.40

BRASS CURTAIN RINGS.

183. ⅜ inch. 184. ½ inch.

185. ⅝ inch. 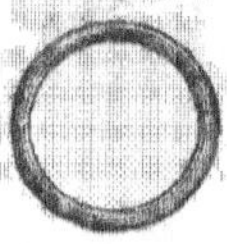 186. ¾ inch.

No.				Per Gt. Gro.
183	⅜ inch in diameter			$1.70
184	½ "	"		1.92
185	⅝ "	"		2.40
186	¾ "	"		2.80

BRIGHT WIRE CORNICE HOOKS AND EYES.

Packed half gross in a box.

Size.			Per Gross.
2½ inches long			$1.50
3 " "			1.62
3½ " "			1.74
4 " "			1.84
4½ " "			1.96
6 " "			2.16

BRASS CUP HOOKS.

One gross in a box.

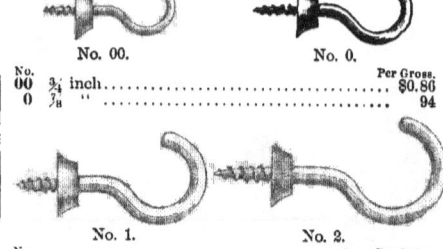

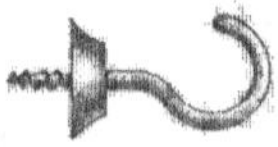

No. 00.  No. 0.

No.			Per Gross.
00	¾ inch		$0.86
0	⅞ "		94

No. 1. No. 2.

No.			Per Gross.
1	1 inch		$1.24
2	1¼ inch		1.28

OIL CLOTH BINDING.

Turned edge.

Packed one dozen sets with corners and pins in a box.

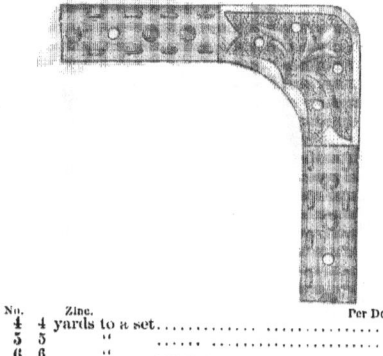

No.	Zinc.		Per Doz. Sets.
4	4 yards to a set		$1.64
5	5 "		2.10
6	6 "		2.52
8	8 "		3.36
	Brass.		
12	4 yards to a set		2.52
15	5 "		3.14
18	6 "		3.78
24	8 "		5.04

BRIGHT WIRE SCREW HOOKS.

Packed half gross in a box.

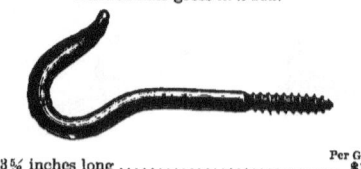

No.			Per Gross.
5	3⅝ inches long		$1.08
7	2⅝ " "		58
11	2¼ " "		44
13	2 " "		36

SEE PERFORATED SLIP AND FRONT PAGES FOR DISCOUNT AND TERMS.

STAIR BUTTONS.

All Packed with Screws, ¼ Gross in a Box.

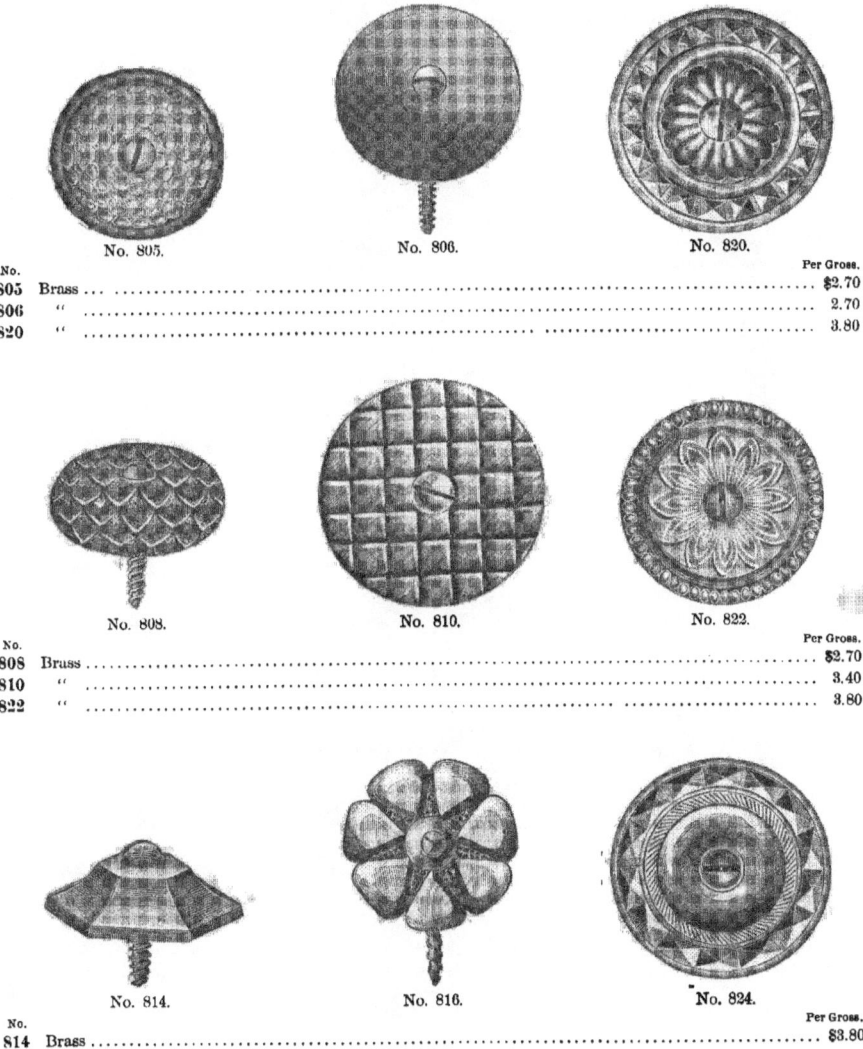

No. 805.   No. 806.   No. 820.

No.			Per Gross.
805	Brass		$2.70
806	"		2.70
820	"		3.80

No. 808.   No. 810.   No. 822.

No.			Per Gross.
808	Brass		$2.70
810	"		3.40
822	"		3.80

No. 814.   No. 816.   No. 824.

No.			Per Gross.
814	Brass		$3.80
816	"		3.20
824	Nickel		4.00

SEE PERFORATED SLIP AND FRONT PAGES FOR DISCOUNT AND TERMS.

INDEX.

NEW YORK JOBBING BRANCH

NATIONAL WALL PAPER CO.

— JOBBERS EXCLUSIVELY IN —

WALL PAPER AND WINDOW SHADES.

416-422 BROOME STREET, COR. OF ELM STREET,

NEW YORK.

www.ingramcontent.com/pod-product-compliance
Lightning Source LLC
Chambersburg PA
CBHW020048030726
47499CB00007B/2643